# Pistachio Head Stories

# What Feels Right,
# Volume One

P.H. Friendly

ISBN: 098882602X
ISBN-13: 9780988826021

# Dedication

For my friends and the togetherness we keep.

# Table of Contents

# Shapes and Parts

Thousands of years ago, Pistachio Heads came into Being when a few good nuts redeployed their genetic potential and became partially, and curiously, human. With skin, blood, guts, muscles, bones, and private parts, P Heads are physically akin to humans, but oddly put together and short in stature. Instead of a cranium, their brain holder is a jumbo-sized endocarp that houses a humanoid brain, a perfectly good brain that is sometimes possessed with nutty ideas. Pistachio Heads (aka P Heads) are a biological and phenomenological wonder, or a freak of nature, depending on who's looking.

Human Bone Heads can't resist being grabbed by the eyeballs; you'll see them fall off curbs and run into telephone poles to stare at P Heads. This hopeless fascination with novelty might presuppose a human affinity with things that are mysterious, magical, or metaphysical, but that's rarely the case. Fear of the unknown usually sets in before any healthy sense of awe can quicken the imagination.

Beings that don't look right or recognizable are certain to rile up the fearful folks. However, one might argue that humans have already accepted as part of their visual vocabulary a wild combination of odd and assorted parts. Ponder, for example, the snoot on an elephant seal, the nose of a proboscis monkey, or the entire platypus. In spite of the mounting evidence that this is a weirdly wonderful universe, Bone Heads are probably going to need plenty of time to process P Heads as a new normal.

But enough about shapes and parts, Pistachio Heads would argue that this kind of palaver misses the point. They prefer to think of themselves as Beings amongst an infinite variety of Beings, as further evidence of a miraculous universe. And hope springs eternal in the heart of every P Head that Bone Heads will someday see beyond their own eyes and deep into the Beingness of the other.

# Chapter One: Halloween

Most P Heads never-never-never spill the beans about their Beingness. It makes the suspicious types crazy. It makes them think that Nut Heads have something to hide.

Mavis Mortimer, Nosy Rosie to her neighbors, gets very determined if she thinks someone has something to hide. She looks and acts like a very proper Bone Head, but is often seen doing unseemly things. Weekdays Mavis is up at dawn to take a tour of the neighborhood. She peeks into trashcans and tries to catch her neighbors in their pajamas. It's mostly disappointing work.

One chilly morning in October she got lucky and saw her first ever P Head. He was wearing a plaid jacket, khaki pants, and white buckskin loafers. His black hair stuck up and out from under a thick layer of pomade.

The little fellow was minding his p's and q's when Mavis charged. She stopped him in his tracks and blurted out, "Your head ... is it a nut?" She knew full well that it was a nut, but she wanted to know why it was his head.

"Good morning, Madam," the little dude beamed. " Isn't it a lovely day?"

Mavis ignored his greeting. "But, what are you?"

"My name is Pete Petrol, and to whom do I have the pleasure of speaking?"

"I'm Mavis Mortimer. And … just what are you and where do you come from?"

Pete smiled, spread his arms in an expansive shrug, and took a bow. "If you must know, I am what I am … from the word go, from day one, from day to day, and from here and now. And for now, if you will kindly excuse me, I must be going, going gone. It was lovely to meet you, Mavis."

Well that's the way it goes with P Heads. Mavis Mortimer was left with her mouth agape. You may think that Nosy Rosie got what she deserved, but without pussyfooting around, she asked the kinds of questions that Bone Heads burn to know.

Mavis rushed right home and rang up her neighbor, Virginia.

"Yes, I have P Heads friends. And yes, their heads are nuts." Virginia sounded exasperated.

"Well, that's strange, isn't it?"

"Only if you are a hard-headed, Bone Headed, Republican." Virginia shot back.

Mavis let that remark about her politics go. "But what do we know about them?"

"That they are eccentric and charming beyond measure."

Mavis paused to collect her thoughts. "But come on, isn't having a nut head a little weird? Does it mean that they are nuts, as in mad or insane, or nuts as in silly and foolish … or that their heads are nuts?"

"They are nutty, not mad or insane, and silly, but not foolish. And yes Mavis, for the second time, it's a nut."

Mavis felt like wringing Virginia's liberal little neck. You could never get a really satisfying and juicy response out of her. It was really maddening. Virginia was always politically correct, avoiding ugly truths. Mavis wanted the scoop and nothing but the scoop, the uglier the better.

*Maybe, P Heads are Martians*, Mavis thought. *They do look a little ET. Maybe there's nothing terrestrial about them.*

"A nut is a nut is a nut, Sister. That's all I got. Info about P Heads is about as rare as a UFO sighting."

Mavis got all sweaty all of a sudden. UFO? *There!* Mavis thought, *Virginia had let it slip. That wily little liberal can't fool me; P Heads are Martians!*

Mavis hung up on Virginia. You can't have a nut head without an extraterrestrial explanation.

Pete Petrol had a premonition that Mavis Mortimer would try to make him as Martian. Bone Heads are always looking for comparisons—it's a this, or a that, or like this because of that, and so on. Pete decided that if he ran into Mavis again he would give her an ET thrill. He'd do his "Doo-Dah and Gone" routine.

Pete saw her the following week. She was all puffed up big as you please, and he couldn't help himself. When he got within a half a block of Mavis, Pete began a frenetic zigzagging left and right while he sang something that sounded like Zip-a-Dee-Doo-Dah.

Pete didn't exactly sing. It was more a recitation in a high-pitched and unwavering tone. He went in and out of his ET routine three times before he was face to face with Mavis.

The *gone* part of Pete Petrol's "Doo-Dah" routine was his pièce de résistance. P Heads can set their legs to spinning so fast that they look like hovercrafts. So when Pete got one stride beyond Mavis he threw his legs into overdrive and z-o-o-m, he disappeared.

His take-off created a gust of wind that lifted the hem of Mavis Mortimer's circle skirt and blew it up over her head. She was wearing her Halloween pumpkin panties.

Pete Petrol didn't want to see Mavis Mortimer's dainties. He wished he hadn't looked back. Sometimes a prank has unintended consequences. His ET routine was a juvenile stunt for a grown Being, but darn, it was good. They didn't call him Pete Petrol for nothing.

Mavis was mortified. Pressing her circle skirt to her thighs, she scurried home and prayed to God that none of the neighbors had seen her pumpkin panties. As soon as she was in the door, she rang up Virginia.

"Be reasonable, Virginia, I've got to know. Are P Heads Martians in disguise or Martian wannabes? Because if they're not Martians I just got punked by a P Head pretending to be a Martian."

∇

Every day is Halloween: proper ladies, Martians, Martian wannabes, P Heads, Republicans and Liberals.

# Chapter Two: Food is Love

Alma said, "Penny Ante has a puny consciousness."

"What kind of consciousness?" Bert asked.

"P for puny consciousness. She's so tight that her buns are sewn together. A peanut butter sandwich at her house is a bread sandwich. Her oyster stew is a sea of grey water. Foods that should be juicy are dry. Foods that should be spicy are bland. If you ask Penny to bring something for a potluck dinner, she brings a tiny tabouli salad, all couscous and no salad. When you have a meal at her house, you go hungry."

Bert said, "Did she grow up poor?"

"No, Bert," Alma said, "no hardship in that family. Nope, this is about a poverty-minded world view and maybe low self esteem."

"Aw quit it!" Bert complained. "This is girl talk. I'm not interested in these kinds of things. Why do I need to know about poverty-mindedness and P for Puny consciousness?"

Alma ignored Bert and went on talking. "It is so un-P Head of her to be P for Puny about life. In spite of being the most unusual of Beings, most P Heads are full to overflowing with generosity and a sense of abundance. My word, over at the P Head Compound, food is love and those folks could love you to death. I never met a P Head that felt P for Puny before. I'm thinking that Penny's nut didn't get nourished somewhere along the way."

Sometimes it takes a dogged determination to get to a plausible understanding of human nature, and it's usually a female who will take the time it takes to figure these things out. Anyway, after a lot of palaver, Alma decided that Penny Ante had missed out on emotional nourishment.

Alma and Penny Ante were neighbors. Alma was a big-boned, hardheaded Bone Head. Even in her old age, she was a workhorse who climbed up and down and all around to scrape, paint, and refurbish her two-story colonial. In the garden, she labored to plant vegetables and hundreds of tulip bulbs. Everything was spiffy and orderly in Alma's world.

Penny Ante spent days on end alone. She was too young to be an old maid, but she acted like one. Winter and summer she wore little print dresses and a shabby shawl. Even in the coldest weather, Penny shivered about the house and yard in her skimpy dresses. Year round, she wore the same industrial-strength oxfords. Nobody, not even Penny's own mommy, paid her much attention. She never looked in the mirror.

Penny lived in a little bungalow surrounded by scrawny shrubs and lots of potted plants that always needed water. Alma and Penny Ante became good neighbors, but because of Penny Ante's P for puny peculiarities, Alma never felt real neighborly. Penny's puniness made Alma think that she didn't care about things in general, and her specifically. And while Alma's cupboards were well stocked and her refrigerator was full to overflowing, Penny's kitchen was Mother Hubbard bare, not that it mattered because she often forgot to eat.

In Alma's world, making food and creating abundance was a way of life, which is why she spent so much time over at the P Head Compound with like-minded others. Over there it was potluck city and Alma was famous for her hearty Seventh-day Adventist casseroles.

Lots of Bone Heads wondered why Penny Ante didn't live *over there* in the P Head Compound. In truth, she felt unworthy. Besides all of those P Head folks were fun-loving and involved, and Penny never felt inclined to communal engagement.

P Head folks were always calling: "Penny dear, please join us on Sunday, my grand pappy is turning ninety. His nut is cracked, but he is still in great shape. He often asks about you. Penny, we know you love to read. We are reading Carl Sandburg's *Rootabaga Stories*. Would you care to join us?"

Penny stopped answering the phone.

It was no to everything until a P Head worker with a nut head the size of a watermelon and a belly like the great pumpkin came to fix her roof. Perry was up on the roof for the better part of a week when it became clear that Penny Ante had taken a shine to that old boy. Early on the seventh day, before Perry came to work, Penny ran down to the corner bakery to pick up a bag of Easy Peasy Lemonade Scones. When she got back, she put a small glass of milk and one Easy Peasy on a plate next to Perry's ladder, and rushed back into the house.

When Perry got to work, he saw her small offering, gobbled it up, and then hauled himself up the ladder. From on high he yelled, "Hey Penny, a guy could starve to death on one puny Peasy. One Easy Peasy is just a teaser. Gimme some Easy Peasies. I waaaaant Peasies. I waaaaant Peasies.

Perry was cracking himself up. His big voice and loud ha-has echoed across the neighbor's rooftops. Alma was in her second-story window, watching him carry on.

Inside her bedroom, Penny Ante was crimson with shame. What were the neighbors going to think? She would have to give him some Peasies to shut him up. She grabbed the goodies and raced outside. Perry was perched atop her hipped roof. He looked like a gargoyle. In that moment, Penny was seized with mirth. In an act that can only be described as uncharacteristic in the extreme, Penny began pitching Easy Peasies at Perry. She had her brother's pitching arm, so scones were flying within his reach and bouncing off his body.

From her upper story window, Alma gasped.

If it was going to be a flying Peasy war, Perry was ready to eat the ammo. He yelled down at Penny, "Right this way to my pie hole." He leaned recklessly in all directions trying to catch Peasies, but his pendulous pumpkin belly finally pitched him sideways, and down he came with a great swoosh. He landed with a branch-breaking crash in a scrawny shrub, on his back and upside down, suspended a mere sixteen inches off the ground.

In another even more uncharacteristic move, Penny Ante began to laugh. It quickly got out of control.

Laughter seized her body and bent it double. She knew that splitting a gut over someone's mishap was not funny, and that made her laugh even harder.

Perry was too stunned to speak. He stared into the sun and saw stars. His heart was pounding wildly. When he could finally focus, he saw Penny, upside-down and peering gleefully into his face. Perry said, "Penny Ante, you make my heart pound. You make me see stars. Will you ... marry me?"

Penny Ante said, "Yes." Just like that: yes.

The next thing Alma announced to Bert was that Perry and Penny had run off to Vegas to get married. When they returned, Alma reported that Penny would be staying put and she knew that because she saw Perry back a big moving van up to the front porch and unload a massive amount of stuff.

Perry brought an abundance of stuff and fun into Penny's life. A month after he moved in, he put a sign over the front door that said: *The Church of Abundant Fun*. Alma and Bert, and other neighbors and friends, started to come around. Perry fed anybody and everybody who came through the door, because that old boy was a proponent of the principle that food is love. Gently, ever so gently, Penny's puny inclinations were transformed. Perry had warmed that scrawny P Head up, and it did her a world of good.

When they got married, Perry asked Penny to drop her maiden name and take his. She became Penny Plenty.

# Chapter Three:
# Everyone Has a Bag of Tricks

"Son, every small town has a bully. Tyson Bennington is ours, and he's a Bone Head doozy. Life is not fair; I want you to stay out of his way." In the face of a clear and present danger, Mommy P put practical wisdom into play.

Peety stomped his feet and yelled at his mother, "I hate being the butt of Tyson's practical jokes!"

On his way out, Peety slammed the back door. Mommy P, who had gone suddenly pale, turned to her sister and said, "Oh Sis, sometimes I'm so afraid. Our P Head boys are Tyson's favorite targets, but Peety in particular. I think it's because he's our little songbird."

Mommy P's Peety was a ten year who l-o-v-e-d Broadway musicals. Unabashed, he went about his everyday activities belting out show tunes in a thin, warbly falsetto. In October, he got to sing *Just a Spoonful of Sugar Makes the Medicine Go Down* at the Elk's Lodge Benefit.

It was Peety's unlucky night because Tyson Bennington was in the audience and he laughed his ass off. Everyone tried to shush him up, but in that moment, Peety wished he had never been born.

In Tyson's bag of tricks you might find things like rotten eggs, worms, baking flour, plastic poo, and live vermin. But he didn't need props for his favorite lunch-time trick.

"Hey, little Sissy, want the rest of my sandwich?" Tyson taunted.

Peety didn't see a sandwich, but he sensed danger. "Ahhhhh ... no thanks, but thanks for asking."

Tyson found Peety's unfailing politeness infuriating. He would wait for it and then pounce—scoop that boy up in a big bear hug, and pull a wedgie. It was pitiful to watch Tyson squeezing the bejeezus out of poor Peety.

Peety's cousin Paley, who'd witnessed this scene one too many times, was outraged and decided to take matters into his own hands. "Peety, Tyson gets you in a bear hug so that he can grab your shorts and give them a yank. It's called a wedgie."

"I didn't know it had a name."

"He's got to get you to give you a wedgie." Paley looked Peety right in the eye. "You ... need to dodge the bully."

"Look," Peety's voice got reedy, "I can't see around corners!"

The boys decided to take Peety's problem to Auntie Patty, who always seemed to know how to fix things. Patty was a potions lady, a homeopathic practitioner. More like an old-time alchemist, she practiced the art of chemical, philosophical, and spiritual transformation.

After the boys gave Auntie Patty all the gory details, she said, "Hmmmmm," and sent them packing. Patty believed that problems were situations that required perspective.

The next day, she went into town to find Tyson. "Excuse me, Mr. Tyson Bennington. My name is Patty. May I have a word with you?"

Tyson, who'd been pitching pennies with friends, interrupted his game and went up to Patty. He towered over her.

"Dearie," Patty began, "I hear that you are sometimes a bit of a trickster, a petty tyrant of sorts. I have a little homeopathic potion to sweeten you up."

Tyson looked confused. "Lady, no disrespect intended, but there is nothing petty, paltry, or piddling about me. And, I'm already sweet! All the girls will tell you that I'm verrrry sweet."

"We know you are a sweetie pie." Patty was benign and positively irresistible. She knew that a healer has to be as small as a homeopathic dose.

"My dear boy, I see that you are sweet as can be, but I am asking you to sweeten up … some more. I have a special sweeten-me-up potion that I made just for you."

"Ha-ha-ha! A sweeten-me-up potion! That's whacked!"

"Are you saying, that you don't believe in homeopathy?" Patty asked.

"No way. I am homeopathic impervious." Tyson was playing to his pals who were within earshot.

"Impervious?" Patty raised an eyebrow. "Well, I dare you, Mr. Impervious. I may be wrong, but if you are impervious you will certainly be able to take my potion, and at the same time resist being sweeter than ever."

Tyson's friends watched in stunned silence.

"Lady, you're on." Tyson announced.

Patty got into her purple purse, pulled out a tiny purple vial, handed it to Tyson and said, "Drink up, down the hatch, here's looking at you, mazel tov, bottoms up, and cheers!"

And, it was bottoms up and down the hatch with Patty's potion. Tyson's friends couldn't believe what they saw.

"Hmmmmm, zesty," Tyson declared, as he turned and walked away.

"Come see me next Thursday afternoon," Patty said, talking to his back. "I live at the edge of town in the pink house with purple rooms. I'll make you some cookies."

The potion was more placebo than potion. *I didn't mislead him*, she reassured herself. She had, of course, misled him, but sometimes, healers have to meddle in the affairs of others for the greater good.

Sweetie pie, that's what Patty started calling him. Every day she'd run into town on some pretext to say, "Hello, Sweetie Pie." Old ladies can get away with that kind of sugar. Tyson's friends snickered. He went curiously silent.

Thereafter on Thursdays, Sweetie Pie would jump on his bike and head out of town to go see Patty. He would sit on the porch with Patty and her P Head friends, act like a perfect gentleman, eat cookies, sip tea, and then leave with a bag of goodies. His friends would never know.

"Auntie Patty, why is Tyson coming out every week for cookies and tea? What'd you say to him?" Paley asked.

"Auntie Patty, I nearly pooed my pants when I saw him coming up the steps. Did you invite him? What happened, Auntie?" Peety was dying to know.

"Why there's nothing to tell, darling boys." Patty had the art of innocence. "I just decided to ask him to come over for cookies. He loves sweets, and doesn't have anyone to bake him cookies."

Wide-eyed and behind Patty's back, Peety and Paley looked at one another and mouthed, "He loves sweets?"

∇

Bless the healers who know how to apply a potion, sidestep a problem, and find a sweetie pie in disguise.

# Chapter Four: OCD Love

Pistachio Heads travel far and wide, from Panama to Pau Pau, Pakistan, and the Pyrenees, looking for a mate with the right stuff—a mate with the wide forehead and pointy chin of a Pistachio Head. Imprinted in their brains is an irrational love of pistachio-shaped craniums. To outsiders this may seem a little in-bred, but that's how P Heads maintain their kind, which is everywhere in short supply.

Patch spent the better part of a year visiting P Head enclaves looking for the Being of his dreams. In Presque Isle County, Michigan, in a small town named Podunk, he met Prudence. She was plump around the middle with a pleasant smile, wide eyes, and a frizzy perm. When Patch saw her, he thought his search was over. For reasons unknowable, he found her frumpy frizziness irresistible. And Prudence looked at Patch with eyes made glad. Everything about him was appealing: his broad forehead, his uneven complexion, and even his ear-to-ear grin, which some folks characterized as oversized.

Patch was a romantic and sentimental guy. Prudence was matter of fact and practical. "Oh Patch, they're lovely, but you don't need to spend good money on flowers. Did you go all the way across town just to buy me purple plums?"

"I want to make you happy," Patch replied.

"But you're always doing things for me ... it makes me feel so guilty."

Aware on some level that romantic notions did not come naturally to Prudence, Patch would sometimes give her prompts. "I love the spotlight of your attention."

"You do?" Prudence said. "Well ... paying attention to you is easy."

"I am glad you think so," Patch said. "I also like the way you lean into me when we walk arm in arm."

"Ohhhh? Well ... I love to lean into you. You're my lean-to guy."

After basking in the glow of Patch's attention, Prudence began to worship the very ground he walked on. And in response, Patch evolved into a lovestruck goner.

But it's hard to relax into happiness. As things should have been getting better for the lovebirds, Prudence, and then Patch, let irrational jealousies, possessive inquisitions, and paroxysms of emotion taint their fine romance. They were lovesick, in the throws of a temporary madness that exhausts its victims and then dumps them back into reality.

Feverish and afraid that he would lose Prudence, Patch proposed marriage. Prudence hesitated a long while and then said, "Yes ... but not now," without offering an explanation.

Patch received 'not now' with a stunned silence. His heart lub-dubbed out of control, a big vein in his right temple started thumping wildly, and his thinking was immediately disordered. He turned on his heels and beat a spastic retreat. Over his shoulder he managed a tight-lipped, "I'll call you from Peoria."

Lovesickness is a roller coaster ride. Patch had been at the top of a giga-coaster rise when Prudence said "yes." "Not now" had hurtled him into a stomach-churning inversion. But, "not now" is not forever, and the logical next question might have been, then when?

After Patch left, Prudence was beside herself. She should have given him some explanation. The last thing she wanted to do was to scare him off. In time, she descended into a pit of self-doubt and loathing. Her shortcomings loomed large: her midriff bulge, her hair that friends called a fright, and her obsession with shopping.

And so it went. Prudence and Patch ached for each other and exchanged long distance phone calls, but to no avail. Patch was afraid to bring up the "not now" issue and Prudence remained silent.

Patch didn't know that Prudence was in the throes of a full-blown approach-avoidance conflict regarding their age difference. She was forty and he was twenty-five. Patch said it didn't matter, but Prudence wasn't sure if she was too old, or if he was too young.

In the midst of all of her suffering, Prudence went to a plastic surgeon for a dermabrasion. Well, technically she had her endocarp sanded with a wire brush and a burr. It was a first for the surgeon, who at the end of the procedure looked like she'd been crop-dusted. Prudence came away with a refreshed surface, but she felt terrible because she knew full well that a shiny endocarp didn't make her any more loveable.

A week later she went to a spa and had her jelly roll wrapped in plastic and her hair straightened, and she still didn't feel loveable.

For his part, Patch was prepared to pretend that everything was hunky-dory. In truth, he felt like a tree, uprooted and lying on its side with all of its roots exposed.

Then one day while Prudence was listening to radio WNMU, she heard Dean Martin sing: "My heart cries for you, sighs for you, dies for you." She dropped what she was doing and ran to the phone. "Patch," she pleaded, "please come back to me." That p.m. he was on the next train to Podunk.

As soon as Prudence saw Patch at the train station, she was seized again with her approach-avoidance conflict. But as soon as Patch wrapped her in his arms, she wanted to be within his reach. Sometimes these kinds of problems get solved in the body—because if the body says yes, it's a go.

As a formality, Prudence and Patch went for premarital counseling with the Podunk P Head Elders. The Elders gently pointed to their age difference and reminded them that love doesn't conquer all. Prudence gave their remarks a long moment of thought and said, "Well, thank you for your concern, but it does for now."

∇

While it lasted, Patch and Prudence lived happily ever after in the moment. Together they achieved a balanced ambivalence.

# Chapter Five: Cold Happiness

In the small town of Arroyo Grande, most folks don't stand out. Perfume Pelissier, a petite P Head does, or I should say did, because locals got used to her P Head peculiarities and then she went away.

During that time, Perfume had pointy parts—a pointy nose and elbows and a couple of big artillery points mid-sternum. In spite of all of those points, she was a softhearted lover of raggedy kids, flea-bitten dogs, and stray cats. Perfume preferred life untended: weeds in the flowerbeds, clothes un-ironed, socks unsorted, and silver tarnished. She was well loved for being the real deal.

Somewhere in her forties, Perfume started acting peculiar. One of her Bone Head pals described her as "a bit inflamed." Because Perfume had a habit of flitting in and out of social encounters, nobody paid much attention when she started smelling a little mustier than usual.

Over time, Perfume's funky smell made folks wrinkle their noses and squint their eyes. The odor got up neighboring noses and stayed there. Perfume seemed oblivious. Had there been other P Heads in her life, mustiness would have been cause for immediate alarm. Alone in a Bone Head world, she was a P Head in peril.

Perfume's polyunsaturated fats had seen fresher days. To be blunt, her fats and oils were going rancid.

And to make matters worse, as fats go rancid, other body parts get inflamed. When parts get inflamed, the ticker goes bad, cells go wild, and sugars go high. Inflammation also causes mood disorders, which is why Perfume was acting a bit overwrought.

Let's face it, Beings occasionally smell bad, but smelling musty and noxious because your fats are decomposing is truly disturbing. Rotting things taste and smell bad so we won't E-A-T them. No one was going to take a bite out of Perfume.

Perfume's friends became concerned, but were reticent to discuss the way she smelled. Finally, someone went to a P Head elder for help. To keep Perfume's nut from going totally rancid, a couple of Elders took charge of the situation. They essentially kidnapped her and shipped her off to Prospect Creek, Alaska. How'd they do that? Well, they gave her a proper scare: "Dearie, you stink to high heaven. You are dead nut meat if we don't get you into cold storage." Imagine … dead nutmeat. Well it didn't take Perfume long to go along. Elders don't bother making nice if a P Head is in peril.

It gets plenty cold in Prospect Creek, Alaska and it stays that way. Perfume didn't go nicely, but once there, her inflammation calmed way down. She realized that she was living in one of the coldest places on earth and that it was populated with other P Heads in various degrees of decomp.

In this new and breathtaking environment, Perfume managed to regain some of her girlish delight. She learned how to throw hot water into the air and watch it freeze, how to wash in snow to toughen up against the cold, how northern lights light up the sky, and how to play pinochle with her new friends. The writer, Wallace Stegner, says that a *placed* person is a lover of "known earth, known weathers, known neighbors—both human and non-human." In such an unlikely place, Perfume became a placed P Head. In the process, all of her pointy parts softened.

Does all this talk about noxious nuts seem indelicate beyond measure? Does airing Perfume's musty laundry strike you as exceptionally bad form? If so, you're probably the type who is embarrassed to tears about your own BO, bad breath, and rotting parts. P Heads would remind you that we are all inching our way to decay.

You may be glad to know that over time Perfume forgot that she was in decomp. She learned how to live happily with the smell of fresh snow, drifting snow, snowstorms, and blizzards blowing.

# Chapter Six: Boot Camp

"Sometimes we stay put because we don't know what to do next. I got a kick in the ass out of there, and I really needed it," Pai told her mother. "Now … I'll be looking for my place in the sun, a primrose path, and a potluck breakfast, lunch, and dinner."

"Really?" Pai's mother viewed her daughter's kangaroo joy with a healthy dose of skepticism.

"Yes, Mom, really!"

In the same month that Pai Pow got laid off from work as a teacher, she got kicked out of her boarding house. With that, Pai Pow, a pint-sized P Head with a perky ponytail and kinetic enthusiasm, piled essentials into her beat-up Pontiac and headed north on Pacific Coast Highway. She said her good-byes, her see-you-when-I-see-yous, and she was gone. The road felt like a blank canvas. Somewhere above Santa Barbara she slipped into a perfect, untroubled happiness.

Past San Simeon, Highway One turns into a serpent that runs high above rugged sea cliffs. Pai took all of the turnouts along the serpent's spine so that she could sit on the edge of the continent and experience awe and wonder. Finally, she reached Big Sur. It felt like home. Pai checked into a rustic one-room cottage, stuffed her belongings into the closet, and headed out for a hike.

Along a wooded trail, Pai met some friendly look-ing Bone Heads and asked, "Are there any P Heads in these parts?"

"None," they said. "But, you'll find Tweedledee and Tweedledum up the trail apiece."

*Yeah, right,* she thought … *but wouldn't that be fun?* Moments later, two identical and rotund young men, of an indeterminate age, dressed like little gentle-men, did appear.

Wide-eyed, Pai sang out, "Hello!"

To Pai's surprise, the boys answered in unison, "Howdjaado and shake hands, shake hands, shake hands. Howdjaado, and state your name and business."

"Wow, that's kinda like Lewis Carroll," Pai sput-tered.

"That's manners!" the boys interrupted in unison.

"You're right," Pai said. "Where are my manners? My name is Pai Pow. I am here on holiday, and how do you do?"

The boys both grabbed Pai's out stretched hand and shook it so hard her perky ponytail flopped around like a beached flounder. "We are Tweedledum and Tweedledee wannabes," they announced.

Dazed by their enthusiasm, Pai asked, "Do you live here, in Big Sur?"

The boys ignored her question. "Can you see the boot prints on our behinds?" They turned around to give her a broad view. "Ha, ha!! We got kicked out of the kitchen. They said not to come back. They said who needs two-for-one jobbers? Boy oh boy, and thank goodness they didn't want us. Thank goodness we got the boot. Sometimes you got to get the boot to get going again."

"Really!" Pai Pow was incredulous. "I believe that. I just got the boot and … and it got me going. That's why I am here. Wow!"

"So, we all got the boot. Do you know what that means? It means we are boot buddies!"

"Where are you staying, Pai? Come stay with us. We live up there … in a big dome. Come stay with us, come stay with us, come stay with us! Please, Please, Please!" The boys hopped up and down in unison. It looked like they were filled with helium.

"And, why don't we throw a party for people who got a move-along the hard way," Tweedledee suggested. "We know everybody in town and every hippie on the mountain!"

That afternoon, Pai moved in with the Tweedle brothers and they immediately started planning the party. The boys made signs and posted them along Highway One. They read:

Ever Got the B-O-O-T?
Come Celebrate the Times You've Pulled
Your Sorry Self up by the Bootstraps.
Party at the Tweedle Brothers, Friday until the cows come home!

Gather with L-O-S-E-R-S who know how to LOSE the past!

Party at the Tweedle Brothers
Friday, until the cows come home

The last sign went over the front door. It said, *Boot Camp for self-identified* L-0-S-E-R-S.

After the signs went up, the new friends sat under a big tree and talked. "Maybe I never want to hang out with anyone, except losers. I'm having so much fun, I need to shake the hand of fate."

"We're with ya, Girlie. In fact, we were genetically designed to roll with the punches." On and on they chattered, and sometimes they were so full of themselves it looked like they were ready to lift off.

When they settled down again, the boys asked, "Pai Pow, what gets you down?"

"Folks who don't know how to play the glad game."

Pai turned the question on the boys. "And what about you guys?"

"Nothing, dear Pai, we were made to float above the fray. We're up on our toes and ready as spaghetti. Ha-ha-ha-ha-ha!!!"

"To be honest," Pai confessed, "even a true Pollyanna like me sometimes gets discouraged. But in your company, I'm glad, glad, glad to be alive. Thank you for being so much fun!"

"You're very welcome, indeed," said Tweedledum.

"You're very welcome, indeed," said Tweedledee at the same time.

And how'd that party turn out? It was a smashing success. People talked about it for years. Everyone gathered in a circle and told "war" stories about breaking through to the other side. For all of the hippies who'd been kicked around by fate and by design, a party that celebrated a kick in the ass was their kind of irony. Everyone stayed and stayed. The Tweedle brothers served three meals a day for three days, until everyone wore themselves out and went home. Pai knew that even without a P Head in sight, she had found her people.

Yes indeed, Pai Pow found her place and stayed put. She lived as a spinster and a sister to the boys until the age of one hundred. Her friends buried her under a magnificent redwood tree that stood high above the Pacific. Three years later, the Tweedle Brothers passed on, in perfect unison, to a higher place.

$$\nabla$$

Blessed are those made buoyant by gladness.

# Chapter Seven: Hoop Dancing

In a snug little bungalow, on a gloomy day, two P Head women sit across from one another at a kitchen table. Talk meanders around everyday happenings and people in common, but it mostly goes where it will. Small hands smooth the tablecloth, fold and refold the napkins, and straighten spoons. Things never get solved, just smoothed out.

Polly is thirty and Pita is thirty years older. The younger P Head is polished and obsessed with her image; the older one never polishes anything except her pots and pans.

It's good to have an older friend when things get complicated. "Pita … I have a problem. My Bone Head pals often act disappointed by what I do or don't do. If I say no when I mean no, take an opposing view, or show up late, I am bound to hurt someone's feelings."

"Why don't you give me an example?" Pita asked.

"I told my Bone Head pals, 'No thanks, but thank you for asking.' They pressed me to reconsider and I said, 'No, but thanks anyway.' They said, 'Why not?' And finally I said, 'Thanks, but I don't like baseball.' It was downhill from there."

"Whoa! Dear girl, that's un-American. You just can't be that honest in the Bone Head world. You gotta lie," Pita offered.

"You want me to lie?"

"Most Bone Heads think of a little white lie as a bit of diplomacy," Pita offered. "You might have said, 'Sorry, I have other plans.'"

"Yikes," Polly said, "How many times can I tell my friends that I have plans before I am in t-r-o-u-b-l-e?"

"Belonging is a dance. Come with me," Pita said. Polly followed Pita out the back door, across the back yard, and down into a small patio that looked like an amphitheater. On the ground, in the middle of the patio, lay carefully arranged hoops. A chair and a boom box were placed off to the side.

Pita pointed Polly to the chair and said, "Sit down, close your eyes and listen. Keep your eyes closed until you feel the beat of the drums resonate in your heart." Polly closed her eyes and Pita turned on the music.

A steady drum beat and Native American chanting filled the space. Holding her body erect and slightly forward, Pita moved her feet in time with the music. She danced into a hoop and stepped on an edge to flip it up. With one opposing leg, and then the other, she moved the hoop up into her hands and over her head. Within a matter of minutes, six hoops were in motion all at once. Pita danced in and out of the hoops, jumped through them, looped them together, and configured them into ever-changing forms.

Polly's peepers were wide open with astonishment by the time Pita picked up her first hoop. That a P Head of Pita's age would hoop it up was one thing. But, that she would abandon herself, let her head bobble, look blissed out and, at the same time, keep her impossibly small feet in perpetual motion, all seemed insanely incongruous.

Polly bit her lips, pinched her cheeks, and crossed her arms and legs to hold back laughter. She was not given to hilarity of any kind, but this … this was hilarious. And because laughter can be its own kind of seizure, Polly's paroxysm went full-blown: she laughed until she cried, kicked her feet, slapped her thighs, and peed her polyester pants.

Pita, whose concentration had been masterful in the face of all this carrying on, finally brought the hoops to the ground. "Now, what's so darn funny?" she asked.

Polly wanted to shout "Everything!" but thought better of it.

"Dearie, I am trying to make a point here. You missed the point." Pita said.

"What point?" Polly collected herself. "Have you gone native? Ha-ha-ha!"

By then, Pita was a tad annoyed. *Ok*, she thought, *it is what it is. Polly is still a puppy. I'll spare her the real me for now and give her back my old, comfortable, and predictable self.*

When they retuned to the house, Polly blurted out, "Pita, I am sorry I laughed. It was just so off the wall … so totally unexpected. Where did you learn to hoop dance … and what's the point?"

"In the 1960's my family lived in Albuquerque and all of us kids had hula hoops," Pita explained. "I learned to hoop dance by watching my Pueblo friends.

34

"The Lakota chief, Black Elk, said, 'Everything an Indian does is in a circle.' Hoop dancing is an expression of that idea. Staying in the circle with others is a beautiful thing, if it's done with the right spirit.

"But enough about me," Pita said. "Where were *you* raised anyway?"

"I was raised in Marin County—and definitely out of the loop," Polly admitted. " My folks were hippies. They believed in live-and-let- live, but that wasn't applied across the board. For example, they would never have danced to stay in relationship with a capitalist pig."

Polly jumped up and started pacing, back and forth. Her pointy purple pumps matched the purple walls in Pita's kitchen. "So, you think I need to jump through a few hoops for my friends? But, how many hoops can a hoop dancer keep in the air at one time? And if you drop one, do they all fall?"

"You can't please or appease everyone. There are limits. And, if you decide to dance, there will be those who don't like the way you dance. Some folks are big black holes of expectations—you'll never make them happy. Dropping a hoop is like dropping the ball; you pick it up again. And yes, you are expected to keep the hoops in the air, but you get to decide when to put them down … when enough is enough."

Polly pressed on, "Bone Heads act like I owe them something."

"Protest all you like," Pita insisted, "jumping through hoops saves appearances. Learn to save appearances is all I'm saying. Perform a little and begrudge no one the effort it takes. Besides, is a bit of a performance really too much to ask?"

"If they need a performance, I am not their person," Polly declared.

"So, you're a person?"

"No, I'm a P Head. OMG! Do you think I'm losing my nut?"

"No. But what are you trying to hold onto?"

"My P Head peculiarities."

"Not everyone will find your P Head peculiarities adorable."

"I don't need to be adorable," Polly countered.

The women sat in silence for several minutes. Finally, Polly said, "Pita … why are all of the rooms in your house some shade of purple?"

"Purple is my favorite P word."

"*That* is adorable."

# Chapter Eight:
# What Feels Right

Priscilla, a perpetually curious twelve-year-old, took all of her questions about life to her Auntie Puddin because Puddin never acted like there was stuff that she was too young to understand.

"Auntie Puddin, I heard Pauly tell his wife Pitty that she was all head and no heart."

"Really? Well, honey bunny, Pauly may be saying that she is a bit too analytical—that she relies too much on reason."

"Oh. Is reason good or bad?"

"Well, sometimes my analytical mind is quite the smarty-pants, a real know it all."

"Your smarty ... pants?"

Puddin, who was old and used to talking out loud to herself, was talking over Priscilla's P Head. "Being analytical is useful, but it's not the only way to make sense of things. The poet, Emily Dickinson, said, 'Much madness is the divinest sense.' She may have been talking about crazy wisdom."

"Wisdom is crazy?"

"Never mind. I want you to meet Professor Poop, and then you'll see what I mean. That old P Head is off his nut, but full of wisdom. You can go over there tomorrow. Tell him that I sent you and that you want to talk crazy."

"Is that the right thing to say to a crazy person?"

"Pricilla, take the back road up to the summit and then drop down into the hollow. You'll see his house in a sea of sweet peas."

"Geeeez, who cares about crazy wisdom?"

"Never mind, take your pals and go see Professor Poop."

The next day Priscilla and two of her friends did just that. Professor Poop's wife, Pia, saw the girls coming up over the ridge and by the time they reached the front porch she had laid out peanut butter cookies and a pot of peppermint tea. The porch overlooked Pia's pride and joy, a grand display of sweet peas in full bloom. The girls felt giddy with the spectacle and the floral berriness of the sweet peas.

After a bit of polite conversation, Priscilla asked if Professor Poop was at home. "Oh yes, I'll take you to his laboratory. My Mr. Poop is a master perfumer. His colleagues call him *le nez*, the nose."

Professor Poop's out-building stood at the end of a long winding path. Mrs. Poop and the girls entered through a tunnel-like hallway into a large room lined with shelves that were filled with bottles of essences, oils, and tinctures. Large mixing bowls, glass funnels, measuring containers, pipettes, and flacons littered Professor Poop's workspace. It was hot and close.

The girls were more than a little surprised when Mrs. Poop calmly leaned over Mr. Poop's work table and said "Come on out Poop, you have company."

Priscilla's friend blurted out, "Why is he under the table?"

"He likes it under there. Poop claims to have pebbles loose in his head. He goes under there to settle his pebbles."

From under the table Poop exclaimed, "But it wasn't until the pebbles got loose that I started to make sense of things."

The professor scooted out from under the table on all fours. From that position, he supported himself on one hand, flipped a half spin and popped upright. "What'll it be girls, straight talk or crazy?"

"Straight talk will be fine," Priscilla said. She didn't want to encourage too much craziness.

"Did you know that my nose knows more odors than I can name? Breathe and smell, breathe and smell; I cannot not smell when I breathe. Did you know that odors put you at a loss for words—that the sense of smell is called the mute sense?"

The Professor's nostrils quivered as he approached his samples.

"Get a whiff of these essences: orange blossoms, roses, and jasmine. Do you like jonquils or plumerias? Want the ultimate treat? Sniff my sweet pea fragrance." Before long, the girls had stuffy noses and light heads.

Suddenly, Professor Poop announced that he was too pooped to pop and that it was time for a nap. In the blink of an eye he was back under the table, from which soon came an audible snoring.

Mrs. Poop suggested that the girls finish off her peanut butter cookies before they headed home. On the way out of the laboratory, Priscilla pinched a vial of Professor Poop's sweet pea perfume and stuffed it in her pocket. Nobody saw her take it.

Back at Auntie Puddin's house, Priscilla confessed. Puddin could not have been more stunned. "You purloined Professor Poop's perfume?"

"I wanted to smell like sweet peas. I am tired of smelling nutty. Last week, Billy Bones came up to me after class and whispered in my ear, 'Hmmmm, nice and nutty.' He told me that he would take a bite out of my head if he had some salt."

"You can't cover up your nuttiness, Dearie. Over phooey under hooey doesn't work."

"What?"

"You are what you are."

"Right, I am a twelve year old who wants to smell like sweet peas."

"We are going to go right back over to Professor Poop's place. You will give him back his perfume and apologize."

"Scent doesn't belong to anyone." Priscilla was defiant.

"Your own nutty scent is attached to you, and you own it. That flacon of perfume was attached to Professor Poop. He distilled it, put it in his bottle, and left it on his table. He owns it."

"Sweet peas are free!"

"If that perfume was free, why did you sneak out with it?" Puddin appreciated Priscilla's logic, but she was not going to lose this argument.

"Priscilla, doing the right thing is a feel. Things in this world get attached. It's your responsibility to figure out what is attached to whom."

Puddin went with Priscilla to see Professor Poop, and waited outside as she sheepishly entered his laboratory.

"Hi, Professor Poop, can we talk ... crazy?"

"You betcha!"

"I stole your sweet pea perfume. I'm bringing it back. It was a crazy thing to do."

"Hmmm ..." Professor Poop nodded and looked grave.

"I took it, but it doesn't smell as good as the sweet peas in your garden."

"Well Priscilla, I guess you could say that I pinched it from God—that I stole His splendor. I've pulled the petals off thousands of sweet peas because I wanted their fragrance all to myself and for all time."

"Auntie Puddin says that if something is attached to someone it doesn't belong to you. So ... you're saying that the flowers belonged to ... to God?"

"Yep." Professor Poop stared straight ahead.

"How does stealing God's splendor make you feel, Professor Poop?"

"Well, now that we are having this little chat, not so good."

"So you are going to pull the heads off thousands of sweet peas again this year? That would be like Billy Bones, harvesting my head—salting and eating my head."

"What?" Professor Poop looked confused.

"Wow, Professor Poop, I am really sorry that I stole from you and that you stole from God. I am sorry to be in on this. It doesn't feel right. Auntie Puddin says that doing the right thing is a feel."

"Ahhh … she's right of course." Professor Poop smiled.

"Professor Poop, is this crazy talk?"

"No, dear, it is not."

$$\nabla$$

Every year thereafter sweet peas mixed with other native flowering plants were allowed to grow wild and glorious over every inch of the Poop estate. People came from all over the world to see the glory and to inhale the mixed essences. What belonged to God now belongs to everyone. It feels right.

# Chapter Nine: To P or not to P

Paulo is a pallid, P Headed geek, a palaverer and a parabolist with peculiar tastes. He has lots of cool friends at High-Tec High who tolerate his peculiarities because he's a very amusing dude. Mostly he keeps his geek at bay, but with his friend Ben he is what he is. In fact, because Ben is the coolest Bone Head ever, Paulo takes a bit of perverse pleasure in geeking him out.

After school Paulo and Ben sometimes hang out at Ben's house because nobody's home. Paulo tells Ben stories, and sometimes his palavering goes too far.

"Hey Ben, want me to tell you a story?" Paulo offered.

Ben, a blond surfer dude, leaned way back in his dad's recliner, propped his feet up and said, "I should put my foot down, tell you to put a cork in it—but perish the thought. Palaver away."

"Ha! You seem to be developing a taste for my stories and a penchant for p words. I must be rubbing off on you.

"So," Paulo began, "last week I went with my folks to this dinner theater in Point Loma. When we got there, the room was filled with old Bone Heads sitting at large round tables sipping port and fruit liqueurs while they waited for the show to begin. Lots of the women looked like little birds perched together for the night. My mom called them *hairdo ladies* because they all wore the same *do, a* bouffant, backcombed bubble fixed in place with a ton of hairspray. Dressed to impress, the hairdo ladies wore evening gowns and rhinestones. Some of them had wrapped themselves against the evening chill in little fur stoles. And, they looked like nesting birds.

"We went there to hear an old songbird, Miriam Gottasong." Paulo explained. "She's the Yankee Doodle Diva."

"What's a diva?" Ben asked.

"A diva, my friend, is a splendid female singer with lots of pizzazz."

"A Bone Head or a P Head?"

"Bone. There are no P Head divas," Paulo answered. "When the Yankee Doodle Diva appeared on stage, she was a patriotic spectacle in red, white, and Prussian blue sequins—a mountain of a woman with a mile-high hairdo at the summit. Miriam belted out a bunch of show tunes and a few patriotic numbers in a big-bodied voice that left all the little birds aquiver. The audience gave her a standing ovation, and as the applause died down, Miriam attempted a grand exit. She picked up the hem of her dress, puffed herself up, and paraded through the audience with a big swoosh. Midway, and in the blink of an eye, the Yankee Doodle Diva went down! It sounded like a sonic boom. Glasses rattled and the birds went, *Ohhhhhh*! Miriam disappeared between the tables, and in the hushed silence that followed, it seemed like she was down for the count." Paulo paused and looked serious.

"The diva took a dive … and what?" Ben asked.

Paulo explained, "Well, it took ten gentlemen to get her upright, but once she was up, Miriam popped back to life with everything intact … including that hair-do which held the summit like an ice cap. She marched right back up on stage and performed a second encore of *Yankee Doodle Dandy*. The little birds were pleased as punch. They clapped, cheered, wept, and waved little American flags."

"Why are you telling me all of this cornball stuff, you little geek?"

Paulo ignored Ben's disdain. "I like cornball stuff, divas, and dames with pizzazz. Are divas and dames not cool or hip enough for you, Benny boy? Because to be cool or not to be cool is the question. That diva was the real McCoy. She had to know that wearing a mile high beehive was passé and she did it anyway! That she was so outrageously, so blatantly herself made her kind of loveable—that and the diva rising bit."

"I wouldn't be caught dead with divas or dames," Ben said.

"Exactly, because you're too cool," Paulo said. "You really are the coolest cat I know. But maybe you're just a category of folks, a type amongst other types. All those old birds had the same hairdos. They're all of a type and with no apologies. Are they perchance cool?"

"Dude, apologize to me for this profuse and idle talk," Ben said.

"Benny Boy, what does a guy like you have to do to be cool? Are you always looking over your shoulder to see what the hipsters are doin' and wearin'? And don't you have to get down with all the right body language and lingo?"

Ben, who was always very self-conscious about being cool, popped his chair upright, jumped out of it, and grabbed Paulo by the scruff of his shirt. In a tight little voice he said, "I don't have to do nothing."

Paulo, with his legs peddling air, sputtered to have his final say on the subject. "Right, right! Being cool is not trying. I'll bet all kinds of folks wake up in the morning and never give the 'gotta be cool' question a thought. Maybe you, me, the divas and dames can all be cool without trying." Ben dropped Paulo, the very pallid palaverer, and started laughing.

Paulo stood up, regained his dignity and said, "Maybe, to palaver or not to palaver is a point worth pondering."

"Seriously Dude," Ben replied, "you need to ponder your geekness."

# Chapter Ten: Love Made Visual

Dr. Palpate didn't mince words. When he got worried about his patients, he let them know it, in no uncertain terms. He made disease processes visual with pictures of things like clogged arteries, diabetic ulcers, and rotten teeth. And the pictures scared the bejeezus out of folks because a picture is still worth a thousand words.

With youngsters, he'd ask for permission from parents before he used his pictures. It took some doing. "Oh no, Dr. Palpate, I don't want you to scare my Johnny with those pictures."

"Ahhh, Mrs. Jones, your Johnny is scaring me and he'll be scaring you before long." Parents always gave in.

"Buddy Boy, what do you see in this picture?"

"Arteries for blood, Dr. Palpate."

"What do you see in this picture?"

"Euuuuh, yuk! Are those arteries? What's wrong with them?"

"Cholesterol, old boy. All that flaky stuff is junk food turned into plaque! And that's what your vessels are going to look like before too long. People get very sick when their veins and arteries get gummed up. But your teeth will probably fall out before that happens because of all that sugar you eat. Buddy Boy, I'm worried about you."

Buddy Boy looked at Doc with eyes wide open.

Well, ouch. Are you thinking, *what kind of a doctor is this*? Dr. Palpate is a P Head and a board certified internist, with a specialty in nut heads, which he didn't pick up in medical school. As for his bedside manner, you may call it as you see it—blunt. He didn't pick that up at medical school either.

Because folks love and trust him, P Heads and Bone Heads alike flock to Dr. Palpate's practice. And, because he looks so open-faced, his Bone Head patients sometimes sneak in a few off-topic questions.

"Tell me Doc, do your kind ... ah, mix with human folks?

"Mr. Jessup, do you mean mix with ... as in mate?"

"Well ... yeah."

"No, we don't. Not that we are opposed to mixed marriages, but we want to keep the old P Head line going, which is why we believe in big families."

"I guess the Pratts are doing a pretty good job of propagating P Heads."

"Yep, ten kids in fifteen years, and I delivered every one. I'm making a house call there today. Mrs. Pratt just gave birth to a baby girl."

That afternoon, Dr. Palpate drove out to the Pratt Plantation. He would check the baby, have a quick look at the kids, and with any luck, he'd find an opportunity to chat-up Mrs. Pratt's mother, Palmira.

"Yay, yay, Dr. Palpate is here." The children gave him a mayhem welcome: noisy glee, up and down joy, and lots of pushing and shoving.

Upon examination, Mrs. Pratt's baby looked like a plump pumpkin, but six of the older children had a bit of powdery mildew in their scalps and between their toes. Dr. P pulled out a picture of powdery mildew that was in full bloom on a pumpkin plant, and showed it to the kids. "I know you guys aren't pumpkin heads, but the same thing can happen to you if you don't remember to dry between your toes and behind your ears. Our ancestors, the trees, are very prone to fungus infections and so are we."

Mommy Pratt nodded and rocked the baby. Doc had her permission to instill in her children a good, healthy respect for the nature of things.

In the window, behind Mrs. Pratt's rocker, the curtain moved.

The ever-elusive Palmira was nowhere in sight. Doc figured he'd have to ask if she was at home. As if she'd read his mind, Mrs. Pratt got up and said, "Doc, I'll tell mom that you're here."

When Palmira saw Doc through the crack in the curtain, she rushed back upstairs to her room to make herself presentable. In her haste, the hairbrush became hopelessly entangled in her thick and unruly hair. To make matters worse, her shirt was stained with paint and perspiration, and her bare feet looked like they belonged to a barefoot runner. Making nice for a gentleman was, she decided, more than she could manage.

"Mom, where are you? Doc is here."

Panic. The hairbrush would not budge, and now she was sweating to beat the band.

Palmira heard her grandkids running wildly up the stairs. She grabbed a big pair of pinking shears from her sewing table and cut the brush out of her hair. The brush and a huge hairball fell to the floor. "Oops!"

The children burst in. "Come on, Grammy. Hurry up."

P Heads are not, as a rule, vain, but in affairs of the heart they are all too human. Ready or not, Palmira thought, I have to make an entrance.

As she stepped out onto the front porch, the kids and the dogs swarmed all over her. When things calmed down, the younger ones cried out: "Gram, what happened to your hair?" "Why is it so short on that one side?"

"Shush, you'll hurt her feelings."

Palmira cringed.

Doc jumped up and said, "Hello, Palmira. You look lovely as usual. You must be an artist who loves asymmetry."

"Well, thank you Doc, but asymmetry is not what I had in mind."

"We'll fix it Gram," the older girls suggested.

*OK*, Palmira thought to herself, *it's too late now.* "Go get my pinking shears. They're on my dresser."

With great enthusiasm, the kids set up a beauty parlor on the porch and Palmira sat down to be sheared. All the long hair that was given to tangles went wildly curly when it was cut.

The girls stuck wildflowers in her springy curls and started shrieking, "Gram's a garden." The dogs tried to sit in her lap. The baby cooed. And suddenly, Palmira felt right with the world.

Doc, who had been watching from the sidelines, said, "Palmira, being loved by children and animals makes you even more beautiful."

Grammy blushed, jumped up, tripped over the dogs, and landed sideways in a heap. Before anyone could respond, she sprang to her feet, pulled an about-face, and disappeared. Everyone stood in stunned silence.

Palmira's daughter ran after her. "Mom? Are you ok?"

"No, I am a perfect disaster."

"A disaster?"

"I am a foolish old P Head."

"Mom, you like him don't you?"

"Who?"

"Him, Doc. You like him."

"Yes, ok, yes! But I am a fool."

Doc was left puddled. When he and Palmira were together, there were always minor mishaps that invariably sent her into hiding. Like that time she fell off the dock in her party dress, or when she split the inner seam of her riding pants, from cuff to cuff. And after that mini tornado pulled all the bobby pins out of her French twist, Palmira disappeared for a month. Nobody ever laughed at her, but sometimes it took all of Doc's might not to crack up. Even her pratfalls were hilarious. Palmira was so painfully real.

An abnormally straightforward fellow, Doc was left speechless. A week later, he walked out to see Palmira.

It took him over an hour, time he needed to think about what he was going to say. When he reached the house, it looked like no one was at home. He walked around back and found Palmira sitting in the sun with a green papaya peel mask on her face and pin curls in her hair.

"Darn you, Doc."

"Palmira, I, I'm sorry …"

"Never mind, my name is mud." And with that declaration, Palmira's folding chair jackknifed her forward onto all fours.

Instead of, 'Oh, no!' or 'Are you ok?' Doc laughed out loud and his hearty ha-has reverberated across the lake. Palmira rolled over on her back and together they laughed until they cried. And when the papaya peel mask cracked on Palmira's face they laughed some more.

"It's you, Doc, that makes me play the fool."

"Me?"

"You make me … a nervous ninny."

"Palmira, I can't tell you how happy it makes me to be the source of your endearing antics."

Beneath her green papaya peel mask, Palmira blushed crimson.

$$\nabla$$

May your eyes be made glad by love.

# Chapter Eleven: Bobbing Heads

Bone Head women of a certain age don't do big hair. Not so for Pistachio Head females, who let wind, and weather, and nature have their way with hair. Auntie Pink, a pudgy P Head well beyond her prime, plans on taking her big, red, and electric hair to her grave.

Auntie Pink has a big heart and big kazoos. Regarding the kazoos, her own cats, Ruby and Agnes and their many cat friends, find this feature a perfect perch, a way to be eyeball-to-eyeball with the one they love. While Auntie Pink never had children of her own, she is inclined to mothering and the healing arts.

Living an ordinary life in a small P Head enclave, Auntie Pink is an Auntie Mame wannabe. In the 1950s the real Auntie Mame is a fictionalized version of somebody's aunt, an eccentric, theatrical, and entertaining woman with *joie de vivre*.

Unlike Mame, Auntie Pink is all work and no play. She thinks that if she can get her hands on enough money, *joie de vivre* will follow. Pink's pal, the Elder Prune, vehemently disagrees. Alarmed by her all-work-and-no-play mentality, he told her outright, "You are a healer of Beings, not a worker bee, and this busy work is getting you nowhere. You act like making money is more important than being a healer."

"Yeah, but, yeah, but ..."

"Don't 'yeah, but' me, Sister," Prune said. "If you give all you've got to making money, money will be all you get. Your big heart is witherin' away as we speak, and it won't plump up again until you acknowledge your true calling."

In truth, Auntie P didn't know how to break the work-for-money cycle. But things started to change when she began taking work as a personal assistant. She'd go into people's homes, spiff up the place, rearrange, organize, purge, and change the vibe. It felt good to get folks organized and to mother them through the process. It felt like healing work.

All of Auntie P's clients had an embarrassment of stuff, loads and loads of stuff that they hung onto for dear life. While her organizational skills made her perfectly suited to help these folks, Auntie P's own personal relationship with stuff was downright embarrassing.

In fact, Pink's house was stuffed to the rafters with stuff that made her feel hopelessly weighed down. If Mame's life was a tribute to living well, Auntie Pink's was the polar opposite.

"Maybe," she told the cats, "I am not and will never be Mame. And if I am not Mame, who am I?"

Auntie Pink slipped into an *I'm not Mame* crisis. It struck hard, and lasted for weeks. With it came a feverish attempt to resurrect her inner Mame. Alas ... she was nowhere to be found.

Auntie Pink began to get rid of her own stuff. She found a single mother who was scraping to get by and gave her all of the furniture in her second bedroom. That bedroom became the only livable space.

Then Persephone Prudhoe moved in next door. The old woman had a halo of wispy white hair that sprouted in tufts from her P Head and a petite figure that made her nut look super-sized. Persephone was charming, but when she started dropping in every day, it got to be too much. Auntie Pink had work to do, and Persephone would not take a hint.

One afternoon Persephone asked, "Auntie Pink, my dear, how many pairs of underpants does one need? Or for that matter, how many sets of dishes, pots and pans, serving pieces, or crafts projects?"

Auntie P sat in shocked silence.

Some minutes later, Persephone piped up again, "Of course, I suppose it's good to be prepared. Prepared to entertain, prepared for holidays, prepared to make things, and prepared to know things …."

Auntie Pink just sat there.

"But I wonder," Persephone mused, "Could Mame have been Mame if she had all of this freaking stuff to maintain?"

"Freaking stuff?" Auntie Pink wanted to weep. "I pride myself on being prepared for every eventuality."

The two of them sat there a few minutes without saying a word.

"OK … I see that most of what I am prepared to achieve will never happen." Auntie Pink began to pace. "At my age, I will never again refinish furniture, make baby blankets, bake breads and cakes, and learn to speak French. I suppose I can get rid of all that sort of stuff."

Over the weeks that followed, some of Auntie's stuff began to disappear. But honestly, it was like moving a mountain. Auntie Pink finally conceded that she was going to be one of those old women living alone with her cats and winding her way through narrow canyons piled high with possessions. Feeling desperate, she dug an old safari tent out of the garage and pitched it in the back yard. She put a chair and a lamp inside and a deck chair outside. Her bed was a futon mattress with lots of pillows and a down comforter. Ruby and Agnes thought it was a cat adventure. When Auntie Pink got home from work she grabbed something to eat and took it outdoors, where she sat until it got dark. "Cats," she said, "I am going to sit here until I know what to do."

Then the unthinkable happened. Auntie Pink's house burned to the ground. Curiously, only the house burned; the surrounding yard looked completely untouched—there wasn't a singed leaf to be found. Everyone was dumbfounded. The cats hid in the trees during the fire, and when it was over, they went back into the tent like nothing had happened. When Auntie Pink got home from work, friends and neighbors rushed to assure her that the cats were safe.

"Just the house?" Auntie Pink kept repeating.

Beyond words, Auntie threw herself down on the ground, kicked her feet, cried, wailed, moaned, and screamed at the top of her lungs. The cats stopped chewing fleas. The birdies went quiet. Friends and neighbors froze.

Persephone walked over to Auntie Pink, crouched down, and said, "Pick up your kazoos and stand tall, Sweetie. Your things had to go bye-bye."

Auntie Pink shot her a dirty look.

"Some of my things were irreplaceable."

"Dearie, you collected all of that stuff in preparation for life, but you were a bit over-prepared. You did a great job, but now you have other work to do and you won't need all that stuff anymore."

Lying flat on her back and looking up at the clouds, Auntie P realized that the wind was picking up ashes and blowing them about. Her things were starting to blow away. She jumped up and walked straight into the center of her burnt-out house. Leaning over, she picked up a handful of the still warm ashes and spread them over her face and arms, in her hair, and behind her knees.

Friends and neighbors gasped.

"There!" Auntie Pink said out loud to her friends. "Dust to dust, ashes to ashes." With that, she headed down to the lake. She walked straight in, clothes and all, leaned back, stretched her arms wide, and floated out to the center of the lake—with barely a ripple.

Word spread from P Head to P Head and from house to house: "Come, the healer is healing herself." And P Head ladies were seen scurrying up the lane. One by one they covered themselves with ashes and slipped quietly into the lake.

For some unknown reason, P Head's heads float. So Auntie Pink was floating out there in the middle of the lake with her flame red hair in a halo around her nut. Pretty soon thirty or more women were out there with her, creating their own hair halos.

For Pistachio Heads, solidarity is not a show, but this occasion created quite a spectacle. From across the lake, Bone Heads started congregating along the shore. "What the heck is going on?" they murmured.

After bobbing about for a good while, the women got out of the water one by one and walked back unceremoniously into their lives. When Auntie P got out, she walked back to her tent, sat down outside, and looked out over the lake. She didn't know what to do, but it didn't matter anymore. "I am not Mame," she told the cats.

∇

Auntie Pink went on to become a beloved healer. As believers in collective healing and to commemorate Auntie Pink's life, the Positively Pewaukeeian P Heads of Wisconsin gather every year in August to reenact *The Day of the Bobbing Heads*. Late in the afternoon, when the lake becomes like glass, hundreds of P Head ladies cover themselves with ashes and quietly get in the water. Across the lake, noisy Pewaukeeian Bone Heads congregate along the shoreline to eat hot dogs and to witness the spectacle. The minute those P Head ladies slip into the water, the Bone Head Peanut gallery gets very, very quiet.

# Chapter Twelve: Going Native

"For better or for worse, I will remain positively identified as Petrus Jacobus Bezuidenhout; Species, Afrikaner; Habitat, Algoa Park, Port Elizabeth ... and must accept the consequences."

Athol Fugard, *A Lesson From Aloes*

Petrus Pistachio, a scruffy little dude in Birkenstocks, likes spending the day out in nature with his Bone Head pals who are biologists and naturalists. With field guides, binoculars, and spotting scopes, they go to inordinate lengths to identify the local flora and fauna. Together they love the ordering principles of biology.

One evening, Petrus and his Bone Head pals went to see Athol Fugard's play, *A Lesson From Aloes*. The play is about the individual, society, and survival. It is also about a species of Aloe that defies taxonomic classification. Afterwards, when the friends discussed the play, Petrus asked, "Wasn't Fugard saying that we have to grow where we're planted?"

A restive silence followed.

Finally, Toby jumped in. "That old Afrikaner, your namesake, grew where he was planted because he knew who he was and where he belonged. I hope you don't take this the wrong way Petrus, old Pal, but where in the world do you animal/vegetable types belong?"

"Yeah," Buzz chimed in. "The old tree of life has no place for an indeterminate species, and that strikes me as a P Head predicament."

Petrus listened politely, but he was more than a little perturbed. Indeterminate? Yikes! And what did Toby mean, where do P Heads belong? Why, don't I belong wherever I happen to be? Do Bone Heads ever question if they b-e-l-o-n-g at the South Pole, on the moon, in subterranean mines, or at breath-sucking altitudes? His pals were really irritating.

With or without friends, Petrus was essentially a loner. Recently, he had begun to wonder if he had taken his solitary pursuits too far. He was hearing a voice in his head that whispered, 'Be a tree, be a tree.' The voice came and went but was especially insistent when he walked alone into the foothills of Petaluma, amongst the oak trees. Curiously, it made his feet itch and tingle.

Having itchy feet was strangely disturbing. Bone Heads get itchy feet when it's time to travel, when they've been in one place for too long. This was not that. Petrus knew that he didn't belong in amongst the oak trees, but he knew he longed to belong. Finally, he went to the P Head Elders for counsel and was referred to I. Promise.

Petrus told I. Promise, "I don't know where I belong or if I have a place in this world. There's a voice in my head that says, 'Be a tree. Be a tree,' over and over again. It's spooky and I think that I'm going crazy."

I. Promise said, "That voice is the call of the wild. After all, our ancestors were trees, meant to be trees, meant to put roots into the earth, and meant to stay put. Now, look here, *be a tree* does not mean that your toes are growing root tips, or that they are being pulled by gravity into the earth. Nope, *be a tree* is a metaphor. It has many meanings, which will be revealed at some point, all in good time, sooner or later—or not, if you don't listen up."

"OK, so I'm not crazy. But where do P Heads belong in the greater scheme of things? Why don't we have a place on the biological tree of life?"

"Yeah, Okay ... we're not a recognized species. Sorry, but I can't get too concerned on that account. Lots of beings still remain unidentified or unknown to science. Taxonomy can only classify and name living things. It can't bring Beings into life-sustaining relatedness. It can't establish a social-sympathetic relationship amongst those Beings."

"Social-sympathetic ... what?"

"I am saying that science can describe and organize living things, but it can't hold those things together in life-sustaining relationships."

"Ok, I see your point. Trees know how to stand together. But, I mostly stand alone."

"Sometimes P Heads think that they can go it alone. They are mistaken. When push comes to shove, we need to get planted in the vicinity of others."

"Petaluma oak trees and Bone Heads seem to know their place in the world. Where do I get that kind of knowing?"

"Why, you can get it everywhere and anywhere you end up. But, for optimal growth, and here's the rub, we all have places and Beings with whom we experience optimal growth—where we have berry red cheeks and plenty of pep, power, and potency.

"But is that a particular place?" Petrus asked.

"Yes, and no. It can be a specific place or it can be a state of mind. Sometimes, we have to grow where we are planted.

"Petrus ... to hear the call of the wild is a good omen. If you heed that call, you will find your way."

"Sometimes I feel like every tree, a stand of trees, an orchard. At other times, I feel animal or vegetable in spirit, and in many forms. Is that the call?"

"That's it. Now, what's all the fuss about?"

"Sometimes, I lose myself."

"If that happens, I'll come looking for you."

# Chapter Thirteen: Up A Tree

Drop-bys, -ins, -overs, and -ups are welcome. Getting there is a bit daunting, but it's part of the fun. Birds and bugs and critters come and go as they please.

Paden was dying to get there. His mother drew him a map: take Pear Lane to the crossing, turn right up Pomegranate Road and look for a big tree that stands at the end of a dirt road. He knew he had the right tree when he spotted a ginormous oak with huge outreaching limbs and a thick canopy of leaves. When he got up close, he saw a sign that read: *P the P lives in this Tree.* Next to the sign there was a gong as big as Paden's head. He banged on it.

From on high, the Elder Pierre the Pontificator boomed down, "Who gonged?"

"It's me, Paden. Is it okay if I come up and see your tree house?"

"Yep, I've been expecting you. Step onto my lift and *Hang on Sloopy, hang on.*"

Paden didn't know who Sloopy was, but he jumped on board and hung on for dear life. The platform inched and swayed up to the tree house's first level.

Paden hopped off the lift and snatched the railing. "Hey, this is great …"

"Yessiree. It's just right for me and the birds and the bugs. Let me show you around."

Surrounded by twisting branches and foliage, the house looked like it had been built by a drugged-out hippie. Wildly irregular walls, ceilings, and alcoves made it look like a fun zone. The afternoon sun streamed in through windows and cast magical patterns on the walls. Overstuffed furniture welcomed a comfy sit-down. It was a child's delight.

Paden looked around, hung his head out of windows, tried out the easy chairs and finally had to ask, "But, Mr. P, where do you poo?"

"Why, I poo in a toilet. Where else?"

"A toilet?"

""Yep, it's up on the next level. It flushes into a holding tank. A septic service comes out here to drain the tank and take the poo away. It works perfectly. Anything else you want to know?"

"Where do you sleep?"

"Why, in my nest, which is also on the next level."

"Can I go up there?"

"Sure, out that door and up, up you go."

To get to the second level, Paden had to wind his way up stairs that wrapped around the main trunk of the tree. In the bedroom, Pierre's bed looked like a nest piled high with pillows and layers of puffy comforters. The windows were wide open and Paden could see all the way to the foothills of the High Sierras. In the bathroom he looked into the toilet.

"Hey, I thought maybe you got lost up there."

"My dad told me that he would build me a tree house, but I don't think this is what he had in mind. Your tree house is really cool. But, Mr. Pontificator, aren't you afraid of … of … falling out of your tree?"

"Heck no. Up here I'm in my element—in touch with our botanical ancestors. *Hang on Sloopy* is my motto. Besides, I also hang tight with my toes like the sapsuckers, the pileated woodpeckers and the pygmy nuthatches. Jump aboard the platform and I'll send you back to earth."

Paden sneaked a peek at Pierre the Pontificator's bare toes and thought to himself, *with those toes a guy could walk up a wall, across the ceiling, and down the other side.*

While Pierre was happy as can be, living in a tree, it was cause for consternation elsewhere. His only daughter and her husband, and the entire P Head community, worried that the very old, and sometimes rickety Mr. Pontificator was too frail to be living alone and on high.

One day a troublesome Bone Head came to call.

"Who gonged?"

"Miss Abigail Aimes."

"What can I do for you, Miss Aimes?"

"You can come down here this minute before you break your neck."

"My neck?"

"Well if not your neck, your nut. I'm here from Adult Protective Services. We got a report that your living conditions are unsafe."

"How nice that you folks are concerned. What kinds of adults do you protect?"

"Well … humans. But, we got a report that you are living in unsafe conditions and we can make you a ward of the court if it looks like nobody's taking care of you."

"You don't say. But, I take care of myself."

"Mr. Pontificator, my neck is getting a crick in it. I must insist that you come down here this minute."

No sooner said than done. Pierre the Pontificator, tucked himself neatly into his escape harness and began to inch his way to earth. He came down silently and directly behind Miss Abigail Aimes, who was still jabbering away about the jurisdiction of Adult Protective Services.

"Boo!"

In one involuntary seizure Miss Abigail Aimes let out an ungodly yelp, jumped straight up and out of her sensible shoes, flung her paperwork in the air, and peed her tightie whities.

"Mr. Pontificator, this, this is simply ... unacceptable."

Swinging gently back and forth in his harness, and grinning from ear to ear, Pierre said, "Miss Aimes, I've come down. Would you like to come up for a spot of tea?"

Mortified, Abigail stood barefoot in her very own wet spot. "Mr. Pontificator, you have not seen the last of me."

Two hours later, "Pappy it's me. Bring me up."

"Pappy, I just talked to a Miss Aimes from Adult Protective Services. She says there will be repercussions if we don't get you out of your tree."

"Daughter, those fancy Bone Heads are trying to pull a fast one. They think that if they can get me out of my tree that they can get their paws on my property. If they knew us better, they would know that we hold property in perpetuity. But let's not go there. I don't want you to worry your pretty little nut."

"But, Pappy, we who love you would like you to come down to earth. And by the way, did you punk Miss Aimes? She seemed very perturbed by what she called your odd sense of humor."

"Dear girl, I am not coming down to earth any time soon. And yes, I punked Miss Aimes—I could not resist."

Miss Abigail Aimes didn't know that Pierre the Pontificator's case had been opened by unscrupulous land developers. As a play-by-the-rules do-gooder, she was a perfect pawn. It was Abigail's job to get that old nut out of his tree, and she would make it happen, by hook or by crook.

A week later Abigail was back with a charm offensive. "Mr. Pontificator, I'd simply love a spot of tea."

"But of course, jump on board the lift and *Hang on Sloopy*."

"Sloopy?" The lift looked like a raft with rails. It made all kinds of groaning sounds on its way up. Abigail was terrified of heights.

"Welcome, Miss Aimes. Do come on board. You can let go of that rail now. One little step and you'll have solid footing. Here, take my arm."

Abigail took his arm. Pierre gave her a boost through the front door then reeled her around and plopped her down into a wide-bottomed papasan chair. Abigail filled the chair to the brim and quickly pinked up.

Before she knew it, they were sipping tea and talking about her own life. And on and on the conversation went for hours until three elderly P Heads ladies came calling. Pierre brought them all up at once, amidst much tittering. The old girls were clearly dolled up, and Abigail thought to herself, *why that old charmer.*

"I must be going, Mr. Pontificator."

"Back to earth then. But won't you come again soon?"

"I'd like that."

When Abigail hit the ground, she felt positively buoyant. She had never had such attentive attention. Why, she had even spilled the beans about being Abigail Aimes. And Mr. Pontificator had asked all the right questions. She looked at her watch and felt a twinge of guilt. *Never mind,* she thought, *I was just softening the old boy up.*

Thereafter, Abigail routinely turned off her cell phone and went up the tree to see Mr. P. She met all of his friends, young and old, and they were lovely. After a while, she started dressing up a bit. She dug out her peacock pin and wore it because she knew Pierre and the P People loved P words and P word animals. She developed a bit of a crush on Pierre. Oh, she knew it was ridiculous—he was, after all, so old and she was so ... large. And then there were all of those charming P Head women who couldn't seem to get enough of his company. Abigail thought how lovely to be so old and loveable and sociable ... and so much fun.

When her supervisor asked her about Pierre's case, Abigail told her that it was ongoing. What she didn't say was that it was ongoing fun.

Two weeks later Abigail's supervisor told her in no uncertain terms, "Get that old P Head out of that tree, pronto. And if you don't take care of this PDQ, I am sending the paddy wagon to get him."

Abigail went to Pierre in tears. She told him that he would have to stand before a judge at the county seat, where it would be determined whether or not he would become a ward of the court and forced out of his tree.

Pierre was strangely calm. He told her, "No problem." And sent her packing.

The next time Abigail went out to see Pierre the sign at the foot of his tree read: P the P Used to Live in this Tree. Abigail thought that he had flown the coop, but two weeks later on his court date, Pierre appeared with his daughter and about fifty P Head friends and relatives.

Abigail's supervisor presented Pierre's case to the judge who, when she was finished, leaned way back in his chair and said, "I always wanted to live in a tree house."

Turning to Mr. Pontificator, the judge asked, "Sir, just how old are you?"

"I don't know. Pistachio Heads celebrate birthdays but not birth years. I could be fairly old."

The judge peered down over his glasses at Pierre. He liked what he saw. The old guy was dressed in a grey three-piece suit, with a tie that read PONTIFICATE in big red letters. He wore Birkenstocks and his toes looked like talons. His white hair grew up and out like an umbrella-crested cockatoo on high alert.

The judge, a live-and-let-live libertarian, took a stern note. "As far as I know, nuts grow in trees. Why shouldn't Mr. Pontificator be living in a tree? Why are you wasting the court's time with this nonsense?"

"Mr. Pontificator, are you a nut or not a nut?"

"Oh, yes sir, I am a nut."

"Then go back up your tree, but I don't want to hear about you falling out of it. I trust you will take my ruling to heart. Case dismissed."

The P Heads, the dubious do-gooders, and the developers filed out of the courtroom. But Miss Abigail Aimes remained frozen in place. She had almost cost the dear Mr. P his TREE. Had her role in this case cost her his friendship—cost her happy days in his company? Noisy sobbing ensued.

And then, he was there, in all of his frail and diminutive glory, sitting next to her, offering a clean white handkerchief. When Abigail's crying and sniffling dried up, Pierre stood up and offered her his arm. She took it. They were by all accounts such unlikely friends.

# Chapter Fourteen:
# The Importance of Mourning

P Pole left the house with a beer and a boogie board. Long and lean for a P Head, Pole wore his board shorts low and his platinum hair down to his shoulders. His bare chest was narrow and leather brown, and his arms and legs looked like twisted sticks. Except for the boogie board, he looked like an old-time surfer.

From behind the curtain in the house next door, the Bone Heads, Lizzy Bea and her mother Eleanor, took notice.

"Lord above Lizzy, who's that? Tsk, tsk, and to think he leaves the house looking like that."

"Aw Mom, that's P Pole, the P Head I was telling you about. He's a great guy."

"Hmmph. Mr. Pole needs to put some clothes on. Is he a bohemian?"

"Don't let his looks fool you, mom, he's really a very classy guy."

"Oh, I can see!"

"No, Mom, looks aside, he is a very genteel fellow who is not afraid to bare his soul. When I told him about poor Auntie Mo, he cried … then we cried together. He cried when Altman clear-cut his property, and said how much he'd miss those trees. He's all over town crying about this and then that. I try to edit out the kinds of things that make P Pole cry."

"Excuse me? Will wonders ever cease?" Eleanor blurted out.

"Now what? Quit spying on the neighbors! Ah, that's P Pole's girlfriend ... or friend. Nobody's sure because she's one of us. Anyway, she's got tons of money and they run around town looking like beach bums."

"Good Lord, what's a woman her age doing in a string bikini? Doesn't she have a beach cover-up? Oh my, she's three feet taller and wider than Mr. Pole. Eeuuwwwwwwwh, I can't believe my eyes!"

By then Lizzy was exasperated with her mother. "Well then, stop looking."

"I can't."

A lot of older women in small town Santa Barbara take exception to P Pole and his lady friend. They think that having achieved a certain age means that you get fully dressed in the morning and stay that way until it's lights out and bedtime.

P Pole goes everywhere looking disreputable and under dressed. But disreputable he is not. With polished elegance, he moves in and out of different social classes within Santa Barbara, and Montecito. For example, he is friends with the fogies at the country club who like to sip Pernod and play poker. When they party, Pole is always invited. Their wives are just horrified when he shows up at their fancy soirées wearing flip flops, a Hawaiian shirt, and his usual bed head. But, there is no denying Pole's charm. He is Santa Barbara's P darling, and the only P Head in town.

The fogies' wives found another reason to dislike P Pole when he started hanging out with Mrs. Stone, an attractive widower, and the sister of one of their own. Mrs. Stone was herself criticized for reckless tastes, for flirting with younger men, and for wearing revealing clothes.

P Pole, with his naked and salty sweatiness, and Mrs. Stone, with her reckless tastes, reminded the ladies that life was not orderly and predictable, which was not to their liking.

But was there more to it? Were these women also uneasy because P Pole and Mrs. Stone inhabited their emotional bodies so shamelessly? Was it because they danced like nobody was looking; attracted attention for their exuberance; took naps in the middle of the day; and cried, sad and happy tears, suddenly and easily?

On a Sunday afternoon, with preparations for a big party underway, Mrs. Stone's sister took them to task. "Oh, for goodness sakes. Are we boo-hoo-ing yet again? What is it this time?"

Mr. Pole pulled himself together and said, "Well … we heard that Joyce lost her precious cat and then we got more bad news about the oil spill. But, don't mind us."

"Mind you? I do mind. My company will be here any minute and weepers are party-poopers."

Mrs. Stone jumped up. "Never mind, never mind. Pole and I prefer the company of folks who know how to live and let live. See you when I see you."

Much later, Sis learned that Mr. Pole and Mrs. Stone left and went down to Milpas Street to party with some local vatos and their families. P Pole is a teetotaler, but Mrs. Stone got pretty pickled. In the wee hours of the morning, the vatos helped Pole load her into the front seat of his Woodie, where she slid like a slug down beneath the dashboard. They had to drag her out and smush her into the back end of his Woodie, alongside the boogie boards.

Always the perfect gentleman, P Pole took Mrs. Stone home, helped get her upstairs, and then spent the night in the guesthouse. The next morning, Mrs. Stone got up at noon and came down to have breakfast with Pole. She looked like the wrath of God, but P Pole seemed completely unfazed by her dreadfulness. When Mrs. Stone's sister came over, she was plenty shocked. *"Lord above*, she thought to herself, *look at the lovebirds*!

"Well, it looks like you two had quite the night." Sis sneered.

"I must have had fun, but I don't remember a thing," Mrs. Stone grinned.

Reports about P Pole, his lady friend, and their exploits began filtering into the P Head enclave in nearby Ojai. Some of the scuttlebutt was dismissed, but questions about Pole's emotional state were especially worrisome. The Elders decided to head down the mountain to see for themselves how P Pole was doing. They met him in Francesca Park, overlooking the city.

"How's life, Pole?" the Elder Puck asked.

"Life's a beach."

"Ah, well good. Our Bone Head friends have quite a lot to say about your … beach," the Elder Poke stammered.

"I've never felt better," Pole announced.

"Folks say that you are quite emotional these days. That seems a little out of character. You would tell us if you were in trouble … right?" the Elder Puck asked.

"Oh, don't worry I'm P Head happy as ever. But, I am in a very emotional place. Most of the Bone Heads that I know think that crying needs to be curtailed … PDQ. But, I am learning to give boo-hoos their due. Lots of tenderhearted folks have retreated from this painful world, and some of them look like emotional flat-liners. Myself, I go surfing to avoid painful realities, but sometimes only a boo-hoo will do."

"But Pole, life is more than a painful reality," the Elder Poke insisted.

"Yes, of course," Pole said. "But, now that I am more in touch with my emotions, life feels more precious. How are Beings going to know what's important if we don't let emotions come into play … if we don't boo-hoo when we feel bad. And there are lots of things worth crying about."

"Emotions can get out of hand. This world can be a sorry place, but we owe it to one another to hold ourselves together," the Elder Puck demurred. "Besides Pole, you can't cry for the world. It's too big."

"Well, your point is well taken, but now that I've opened the floodgates, I feel like crying for some of the things that matter. Sometimes Beings and circumstances need a sympathetic watering. Besides, the waters of sadness drain down and away. And, don't get me wrong, I am also a proponent of happy tears."

"But," the Elder Puck pressed on, "there are Bone Heads who call you and your friend, Mrs. Stone, the boo-hoo lunatics."

"Be that as it may. And, let me put it this way: Mrs. Stone and I know how to hold happiness and sadness in the same container."

"My dear Pole," the Elder Poke softened his voice. "Let me be blunt, we P Heads are known for our positive world view. This is very un-P Head of you. We support your personal choices, and your show of feelings and emotions, but for Pete's sake, tone it down. Why don't you come and live with us at the P Head enclave where life is a bit more … measured?"

"And leave my beach?" Pole said.

"Yes."

"No thanks, guys. Besides, folks out here need someone to cry with. I am that guy. Our emotional lives are my beachhead—my context. We're just getting real together."

"Getting real?" The Elders looked dismayed.

"Thanks for your concern. But, it's human to feel sad. Being human is in my DNA, and I am not afraid to be my human half. I'll come back into the P Head fold if sadness ever gets the best of me … or when there's nothing important left to mourn."

# Chapter Fifteen: Perspectives

Beatrice, a skin and bones Bone Head, pulled on a sweater and stepped outside. From somewhere down by the woods, she heard a faint wa-wa-wa. She walked to the end of the driveway and turned into a wooded grove. The crying came from deep within. Tromp, tromp, tromp … listen … wa-wa-wa. Tromp, tromp … listen. Bony Beatrice felt a motherly panic. Suddenly, the ground began to tremble and she heard the crushing of undergrowth. A moment later a massive body of stampeding pigs appeared out of nowhere and whizzed past her like she wasn't even there. When the dust cleared, she steadied herself and looked around. And there he was, pink and pitiful, a baby pig caught in a live animal trap. Beatrice rushed to free him from the cage. "There, there, darling. You're okay now." The piglet screamed louder than ever. Securing the baby under one arm and dragging the trap behind her so nobody else could use it, Beatrice hurried home.

Beatrice's husband, Fred, was standing on the porch wondering where she'd gone. "What the heck?"

"Fred, meet Wa-Wa. I found him in the woods in this trap, wailing his little heart out. And, I was nearly run over by a pack of pigs."

"What are you going to do with him?"

"Keep him. Somebody was going to make him into bacon. He's probably one of Portley Pistachio's pet pigs. So, I'm going to ask Portley if I can be this one's mommy."

"Give that pig back to Portly or let *us* make him into bacon."

"No flesh, Fred. No bacon. Get it through your head; I'm done eating flesh. And as long as I am the cook, so are you."

"Your new P Head friends are making a food freak out of you," Fred protested.

"If you don't like it, fire the cook."

Wa-Wa went from screaming, to whimpering, to sleep, cradled in Beatrice's arms. "Wa-Wa, you are a darling boy," she cooed. Being a vegetarian made Beatrice feel more tenderhearted toward edible Beings. Presently, she was plenty worried about Wa-Wa's real mother and Portley's other pigs. A couple of times a year, local yokels poached one of Portley's pigs and then had the nerve to host a community pig roast. *And, imagine,* she thought, *setting a trap for a baby—it's just despicable.*

Beatrice was embarrassed to admit that her newfound tenderheartedness did not extend to her husband. Her Fred had turned into a jumbo pork sausage. Not that she didn't appreciate pork on a man, but when food is all he can think about, a wife gets pretty turned off. Where, oh where, Beatrice wondered, is the boy that I married. What to do, what to do—with pig poachers and with my very own Fred?

Beatrice glanced over at her husband and felt a sense of despair. *I guess I love him, but lately I've changed my mind about so many things.* She decided that they needed marriage counseling, and that she would get the ball rolling. Because she so admired the way her P Head friends lived their lives, she decided to ask the Elder Pie for his perspective.

"Elder Pie, this is going to sound awful, but my husband Fred is missing. I assume he is somewhere under all that adipose tissue, but for the life of me I can't find him. He grubs for food all day—his appetite is voracious. He loves food more than he loves me."

"Hmmm." Pie leaned forward to listen.

Beatrice bombarded the Elder Pie with complaints. When she ran out of steam, she asked, "So, what do you think I should do?"

"Well, you know … food is love, so keep on preparing healthy meals for your Fred. And regarding some of his more annoying habits, try to redirect his impulses. But don't pay too much attention to what you don't like about him. You will lose perspective. Edit, my dear Beatrice, edit."

Beatrice's eyes narrowed. "So … redirect and edit?"

"Hmmm," Pie responded.

"Elder Pie, I am not getting any younger except between my ears. My Fred acts old upstairs and down. The man is impervious to change. I want him to digest new ideas and new paradigms. The only thing that Fred digests is food, which goes in one end and comes out the other."

"Never mind. Forget what you think you know about Fred."

Beatrice left with her head spinning. *Redirect, edit, and forget what I know about Fred? Yikes. What kind of namby-pamby, mumbo-jumbo is that?*

Dispirited, Beatrice went over to Portley's house and began to rant and rave about the "red neck" pig poachers and their night raids. Finally it dawned on her that Portley wasn't worked up—at all.

"Hey you, get mad, okay. We need to do something to save your pigs." Beatrice's face felt red and hot. Her bony and cavernous armpits were all sweaty.

"But, Beatrice, ranting and raving isn't my style."

"Well, Mr. Laid Back. How do you characterize your style? And who's going to make those pig rustlers pay? Why don't we lie in wait for them and take a few pot-shots at their butt cracks?"

"I am not into retaliation." Portley said in a small voice.

"Then, whatcha got?"

"Er, well … nothing." Portley admitted.

Beatrice felt a migraine coming on. *Yikes*, she thought, *these namby-pamby P Heads are driving me crazy.*

In fact, Portley was secretly hatching a plan, which he later presented to his wife, Pigeon, for approval. "My dear Pigeon, regarding our precious pigs, I have been very angry with our pig poachers. I have a plan that may effectively redirect my anger, and their dirty deeds. We must avoid confrontation, but I'm not above scaring the poo out of rednecks. For the greater good of God's creatures, there are some human activities that need to be curtailed.

"Pigeon, tomorrow I want you to go into town and start a rumor. Tell folks that we think of our pigs as angelic Beings. And if that seems overblown, or if people look at you like you are nuts, as in mad or insane, then never mind, so be it.

"Oh, and one more thing, you know how Elder Pie says forget what you think you know about folks? Well, after today I am not going to use that term 'redneck' to describe our pig poaching neighbors. It's pejorative poison and I regret my inclination to apply it. And, instead of lumping them together as pig poachers, I will call them by their real names. But regarding my plan, don't tell anyone what we're doing."

Portley had decided to paint his pigs. He didn't like the idea, but he'd use a water-based paint that would wear off, sooner than later, given all the mucking about that pigs do. That afternoon, Portley and Pigeon painted all fifteen pigs, from the top of their heads to the tip of their tails, with a single stripe of white glow-in-the-dark paint. That night, all their potbellied pigs, big and small, glowed starlight blue, not white. And together they looked more alien than angelic. And sometimes, the best-laid plans have unintended outcomes.

The poachers hadn't nailed one of Portley's pigs for a couple of months, and he was worried sick about his little angels. If seeing glowing pigs in the night didn't permanently unnerve his covetous neighbors, he would have to file a complaint with the sheriff.

Every Monday for the next three weeks, Portley went into town to check the Bone Head rumor mill. Finally he heard what he wanted to hear.

The clerk at the post office asked, "Hey, Portley old man, how's it going? By the by, have you seen blue lights out your way. Some folks are talking about squiggly blue lights in the night."

Then Portley ran into Vinnie, the local vet. "Portley, some of our neighbors got lost out near your property the other night and they came home all shaken up. Some of them even peed themselves. What's going on out there?"

In each encounter, Portley was deliberately vague. "Ah, thank you for asking. Me, Pigeon, and the pigs—all my little angels—we're just fine."

It was Beatrice who finally gave Portley the real scoop. "Portly, I've heard some crazy stories lately about those shameless pig poachers. Apparently they followed some pig mutterings deep into your woods and saw a blue glow. As they got closer they saw blue streaks, going in all directions. The streaks looked like lines of electricity with squiggly ends. It scared the hell out of them, and now there are extraterrestrial rumors afloat. Have you seen anything strange? If those dumb rednecks sell this story to the tabloids, you won't have any pig poaching, but you'll have lots of weirdoes out here waiting for the mother ship to come in."

"Extraterrestrials? Omo, Omo! Praise the universe of unintended outcomes," Portley blurted out. "I've got to get going. It's bath time for my little angels."

"And it's dinner time for my Fred. He'll be grunting and grumbling at the trough if I'm late. And, Wa-Wa will be missing his bony mommy. My boys keep me busy."

# Chapter Sixteen: Happiness

Dee said to her friend Flo, "Psychology is always telling us what's wrong with us. It must be because humans can't get anything right."

"My art teacher says that folks are in their right minds when they make art," Flo offered.

"Pshaw! What's a right mind?" Dee sneered.

"A mind that is occupied with a mindful devotion to some principle or process. My P Head friends think that if you're in your right mind you'll do right by the world."

"I don't know any P Heads, but they sound like a bunch of goody two-shoes." Dee's voice had a cutting edge.

"Dee, what makes you so irritable?"

"Maybe it's because you're a beacon of light looking for goodness in a world that is full of P-U-K-E."

Flo slumped down in her chair. *Full of puke? How,* she wondered, *did I ever get to be friends with this woman?*

Determined not to be undermined by Dee's derision, Flo took a deep breath and changed the subject. "Dee, did you know that P Heads call us Bone Heads and that it's not a pejorative? And by the way, I am leaving tomorrow for a weeklong retreat in P-ville. If I can get you a room, would you like to come? It'll be very relaxing and you can meet some of my P Head friends and see for yourself what right-mindedness looks like."

Dee was dubious, but that afternoon she and Flo packed up and headed out to P-ville.

P-ville has a population of about two hundred. The Retreat House, which sits amongst oak trees and next to a large pond, is a two-story brick building that used to be an old school. The rooms, named after different artists, offer the epitome of comfort, but most of the guests prefer to be outdoors on the veranda in big lounge chairs or in the garden that is filled with flowers.

The disdainful and uptight Dee, and the easygoing and frowzy Flo arrived, checked in, and went directly into the garden where they found two comfy chairs under a blooming purple plum tree. As soon as they plopped down, Pilar, a roly-poly P Head and the retreat hostess, appeared with a pot of peach tea and scones with peppermint and crab apple jelly.

Right from the start, Dee was demanding and snappish with Pilar, the housekeepers, and any P Head that crossed her path. The idyllic setting and the staff's attention to detail did nothing to soften Dee's critical spirit. "I prefer my tea piping hot. The scones are stones. My pillows are hard and the comforter on my bed smells like lilacs. I hate lilacs. And, why oh why are there so many P-word foods on the menu?" With unfailing friendliness, and without a trace of irritation, the P Heads bowed and offered their apologies.

"Dee, my dear friend," Flo pleaded, "you are a nit-picking crab cake. Can't you just relax a little?"

Pilar took one look at Dee and had her pegged: the woman was not in her right mind. A week later, she told the kitchen staff that the big, malevolent malcontent in the Van Gogh suite needed meaningful work and would they bring her into the fold. They said, OK, and Pilar was pretty relieved because her P Head patience was running thin.

Dee jumped at the opportunity to be Pilar's kitchen consultant. And consult she did. She stuck her nose into the making and presentation of every pancake, pasta, pizza, pastry cream and peach cobbler. In truth, Dee was very impressed with the P Head cooks, their cuisine and the spotless kitchen, but compliments were completely alien to her nature. She considered critical commentary a far more useful contribution. Dee did, however, possess a loveable helpfulness. "I'd be glad to do that. Never you mind, let me chop those onions. Do you want some help with those dishes?"

In the kitchen, Dee's glasses were smudgy, her sneakers were food-stained, and the sleeves of her cashmere sweaters were soggy. None of that mattered. Dee got P Head happy. She woke up in the morning with purpose, whistled her way to the kitchen, and acted like all was right with the world. When Flo left, Dee extended her stay for another three weeks.

At the end of the fourth week, Pilar said, "Dee, the Van Gogh suite has been reserved for next month, and we don't have any other room to offer you."

"Really? Well, I ... er ... hmmm. I guess I'll have to go home." Pilar offered her apologies, but Dee turned and walked away. Back in her room, she wept bitter tears. "The P Heads are trying to get rid of me. Well, to Hell with them. They, *sob, sob*, are just a bunch of happy … fakers!"

The next day the kitchen P Heads gave Dee a going-away party and thanked her to the heavens for all her help. When it was time for some good-bye hugs, Dee recoiled. Before she could get the hell out of there, an unwitting dishwasher yelled, "Group hug!" and the P Heads swarmed her. Dee turned into a board, but they squeezed away. Towering over them, she grabbed a door jam and pulled herself free. Not that you would ever know it, but Dee was very pleased. And in spite of the fact that her heart was spilling over with emotion, Dee blew out of that party with no more than a breezy, "Ta-ta."

Dee went home and flopped on the couch, pulled a comforter over her head, and stayed there. Flo called and knocked on the door, but Dee pretended that she wasn't home.

On the morning of the third day, Flo and a neighbor climbed in through an open window, expecting to find Dee's corpse.

"You're not dead."

"Too bad, huh?" Dee's lips barely moved.

Two weeks later, Dee was still couch bound, and Flo didn't know what to do with her. She thought about calling County Mental Health, but decided instead to call the Elder P Head Pap whose company Dee had enjoyed while she was at the retreat house. Everything about the Elder Pap was wrinkled: his endocarp, his hide, his clothes, even the palms of his hands, but Pap was famous for ironing out predicaments peculiar to Beings.

The Elder came right over and Flo let him in. "Hi Dee. How's it going?"

"It … is not."

"Hmmm. Is there something troubling you?" the Elder asked.

"I wanted to tell them how much they meant to me and that I admired them."

"Who?" Pap asked.

"The kitchen P Heads."

"Why didn't you?"

"It wouldn't come out. I am a paper-thin cold cut," Dee confessed.

"Hmmmm."

"Is 'Hmmm' all you've got?" Dee demanded.

"What do you need?" Pap asked.

"If I knew, I'd get up and get it myself."

"I'll come again tomorrow," Pap announced.

"Can I show you the door?"

The Elder Pap came back every afternoon thereafter. Each time he brought some of the kitchen staff with him. He let himself in, opened the windows, made tea, and laid out cookies. Off shift, the P Heads chatted away about food, recipes, and kitchen stuff. They completely ignored the inert lump on the couch.

The lump listened.

On the third day, Dee asked, "What are you guys doing here anyway?

"We are going to see you though this." Pap replied.

"This what?"

"This thing that has you under its spell."

"For how long?" Dee asked.

"Until you show us that you care about us."

"Care about YOU? What'll that take?" Dee looked dismayed.

"Well … we'll know it when we see it."

Silence. Dee was thinking—they are nuts after all.

When the P Heads left, Dee got up, shuffled into the bathroom, took a shower, came out and sat down. "Hmmmm, hmmmm," she hummed.

The next day when the Elder Pap and the kitchen P Heads showed up, Dee greeted them at the door and led them to the dining room. The table was set with her mother's silver tea service and china. Atop a glass pedestal sat a magnificent three-layered pound cake, with alternating interstitial spaces filled with a raspberry jam and lemon curd, finished with a butter-cream frosting. The frosting was a baroque flourish of pansies and periwinkles.

It was an altar to friendship, and the P Heads stood before it in awed recognition. And without thinking, Dee broke the spell. "Now for Pete's sake, will you guys stop coming?"

The other P Heads looked stunned, but the Elder Pap spoke right up. "Okey-dokey, Dearie! But don't be a stranger… or we'll be back."

# Chapter Seventeen:
# A Perspicacious Fellow

Phil's a fifteen-year-old eavesdropper who does a lot of shameless skulking about in search of advantageous listening. He dresses like a retro hipster and wears his straight, black hair in a big pompadour that is greased into a fixed and forward position. But that pompadour atop his smallish endocarp doesn't get as much attention as his ears, which look more like ginormous satellite dishes. When fully engaged in listening, they rotate ever so slightly so that if you look at him for too long you start to feel seasick. And if you want Phil's undivided attention, well, forget it, because he is almost always tuned to other people's conversations.

Phil is obsessed with Bone Head talk, which makes him a bit of an embarrassment to other P Heads who make it a point to mind their own business. That said, he has been known to bring back valuable human intelligence—the kind of information that broadens a point-of-view or a subject. It should be noted that Phil is not interested in gossip mongering or snooping. He is instead curious about other ways of being in the world. Phil is listening for ideas.

As unobtrusive as a P Head may wish to be, he always has a trail of gawkers. And, Phil's ears, his high riding pompadour, and his nut head, make him a gawker's delight. In pursuit of listening, Phil must go undercover in oversized hoodies and sunglasses. He is also forced to crouch beneath windows, hover about in hallways, or disappear into bushes. If he gets lucky, folks are too engrossed in their conversation to notice his proximity.

One day, Phil was down on all fours, picking up change, when he overheard an interesting exchange.

Bone Head number one: "The third side in any dispute is worth considering."

Bone Head number two: "I don't have a clue what you are talking about."

Bone Head number one: "You know, my side, your side, and now there's a third side."

Bone Head number two: "But, what side is that?"

Just then an ambulance zoomed down the street with its siren blaring, and Bone Head number one's explanation disappeared into thin air.

Phil knew he was onto something. He ran home and asked his folks what they knew about the third side. They didn't know anything, so he asked his teachers, the neighbors, the day laborers, and passers-by. Nobody knew.

A couple of weeks later, on a sweltering day in the school yard, two Bone Head bullies, Dick and Harry, went head to head and nose to nose. It was an everyday occurrence. It always got ugly.

Dick and Harry were all puffed up and ready to rumble when Phil picked up a counselor's bullhorn and yelled at them, "There's a third side!"

Dick and Harry stopped dead in their tracks and turned to look at Phil.

"Shut up, Phil!"

"Yeah, stay out of this, punk. It's none of your P-ness."

"There's a third side!" he yelled again into the bullhorn. By now, all of the kids in the schoolyard were gathered around—not knowing what to expect.

Phil didn't have a script. He wasn't even sure what the third side meant. He was letting an idea show him the way.

Dick and Harry dropped their dispute and stormed Phil.

"Alright … dumb ass. What's your problem?" Dick demanded.

"Ahh, ahh. Well, we, ah, that is, all of your school-mates, represent the third side … and the collective. We are sick of your bickering and fighting. Our side wants you two to knock it off … to stop ruining our lunch time."

"Butt out P Head."

"Yeah, beat it, or I'll pulverize your nut."

By now the onlookers were three or four deep. They remained curiously silent during Phil's challenge and then someone blurted out, "We are the third side." And others did the same. In the blink of an eye it was monkey see, monkey do when everyone started jumping up and down like Maasai warriors and chant-ing, "We are the third side."

The chanting and jumping created an awesome spectacle that the teachers and counselors failed to appreciate. They had to raise their voices and push their way into the crowd to get them to disperse. By then the kids had their mob minds all revved up, thinking that they were about to have their collective say. They were not easily dissuaded.

Afterwards, the principle was livid. He called Phil into the office. "You are an instigator and a buttinski."

"But I, I was instigating on behalf of the community. That mob was on my side."

"The key words here are mob and instigating. I will not have students instigating uprisings ... never, never, never!"

"But, but ..."

"Never mind, Mister, you worked that crowd and I am calling your folks."

Later, Phil tried to tell his parents what happened. "Mom, Dad, I wasn't speaking for myself, I was speaking for the community ... for the third side."

"Son, how do you know what the community wants?" his father asked. "Do you speak for everyone?"

"Well, no. But, who speaks for the greater good? Everyone is sick of Dick and Harry and their endless troublemaking."

"Sonny," his mother interjected, "we P Heads don't do noisy meddling."

"Maybe I'm mitigating the bystander effect," Phil said.

"'Mitigating by-standers?' Son, you are too smart-alecky for your own good. I am calling the Elder Perspicacious and you will work this out with him."

The Elder Perspicacious lived like trailer trash in a two-room trailer outside the P Head compound, in the redwoods. His trailer smelled dank and moldy, but he himself smelled like Dr. Bronner's soap. Phil wished he was elsewhere.

"So, you've been listening in, eh?" the Elder Perspicacious said.

"Yes," Phil answered in a dispirited voice.

Perspicacious shot him a glance. "Hear anything good?"

"I heard about the third side. Did mom and dad tell you what happened?"

"They did. But, I guess you didn't know that for those who facilitate conflict resolution, the third side is thought of as the surrounding community—community members who try to play an influential and constructive role in a dispute."

"Well … I guess I was acting as a community of one."

"Want some peanut brittle?" Perspicacious asked.

Phil didn't move and silence stretched out between them. Finally, he blurted out, "Don't you have an opinion? I'm a kid after all, aren't you going to tell me what to do?"

"Nope."

"Doesn't being the perspicacious Elder mean that you are supposed to be perceptive and discerning? What've you got? I am in a jam here."

"Peanut brittle? But be careful, because it can break your snags."

"I don't have snags, and I don't eat nuts."

"Oh, we've all got snags."

"Are we talking teeth?" Phil looked dismayed.

"If you want to."

"What's a kid got to do to get a little perspective?"

"Listen with your heart."

"I can't believe you eat nuts. It just seems all wrong."

Crunch, crunch, crunch.

# Chapter Eighteen: People Pleasing

Juicy Jo found Prissy, her P Head neighbor, in her yard bent over and next to a glorious patch of sweet peas. Prissy was nose-to-nose with a gopher.

"What in the world are you doing?" Juicy Jo asked.

"This is a rescue operation," Prissy said. "My neighbor Rosie has a cat that catches gophers and brings them to her doorstep—alive! Rosie takes the gophers away from the cat, and because she doesn't want to kill them, she'll chuck them into her trash.

"Oh …"

"I pulled this one out of Rosie's trash can and thought that he would like to live here in my garden. It looks like we are both terribly fond of sweet peas."

Speechless, Juicy Jo turned and headed for home.

What Prissy didn't tell Juicy Jo was that she had since brokered a deal with the gopher chucker, who agreed to bring all of her cat's gophers over to Prissy's "estate" to live. It was a hush-hush arrangement.

That Prissy will not trap to kill gophers, or mice, sets her up for scorn and ridicule in her neighborhood. It makes Mr. T. Bone Spade furious. "Your gophers go under the street to my house." And Mr. Spade knows this because he sits at his property line and waits for gophers to pop up so that he can lop their heads off with his shovel.

Prissy thinks of her neighborhood as a community and accepts her responsibilities therein. But, after living in and among Bone Heads for thirty years, Prissy is weary of the day-to-day and time-consuming demands of neighbors.

Community is a big deal to P Heads, so it was with a real sense of personal failure that Prissy went to talk to the Elder Plant about her predicament. Prissy wanted the counsel of someone who epitomized community spirit.

"Elder … my neighbors are good people who mostly tolerate my P Head peculiarities, but I am sorry to be so chummy with them. Being amiable makes me look easy and available—like someone you can count on for help. And while I don't mind doing a favor for someone now and then, I certainly don't want to follow up a favor with an obligatory chat over the back fence, a coffee date, or a shopping spree. Nor do I wish to drop in on, or be dropped in on by, anyone."

"Whoa. That's downright unneighborly for a P Head."

"I have a need for independence and solitude and a preference for my own friends. And it pisses folks off."

"But, being helpful is always a good thing," the Elder Plant said.

"Sure, but how much is enough? I have neighbors who stick it to me when they don't get enough of me."

"Stick it to you how?" the Elder plant asked.

"I am snubbed, sidelined, and pummeled with pointed remarks."

"Prissy, ignore that stuff and just be friendly."

"Yeah, right. It's being friendly that keeps me in the thick of things. What would the Buddha do?"

Suddenly, Prissy was on the ground and belly crawling to get in-between two rows of sky-high sweet peas. "Down, I beg you. Elder, get down! If she sees us she'll talk your head off. Lower! Follow me."

"Who? I don't see any one," the Elder Plant protested.

"Shhhhhhh. Hurry!"

"Prissy! This is ridiculous. Just tell her we're busy."

"She doesn't care! She always shows up when I have company. Please," Prissy pleaded.

"Why can't she join us?"

"You don't get it. It'll only encourage her. Shhhhhh, I beg you! Ohhhh, if I was a gopher, I'd be heading for China," Prissy moaned.

The Elder Plant was quite perturbed, but he scooted in between the rows of sweet peas, rolled over on his back and stretched out. *Hmmm,* he thought, *the smell of the earth and flowers.* Prissy, who had burrowed way in ahead of him, was dead quiet.

It was a good ten minutes before Prissy reappeared and declared, "The coast is clear." Beneath the flickering colors and tangled vines, the air was cool and delicious. Prissy and the Elder sat side by side and savored the moment, and before long they picked up their conversation where it left off.

"Prissy, what were you trying to say before we were interrupted?"

"Oh, just that I … I want to be left alone."

Elder Plant looked earnest. "But, you're a P Head, surely community and service are somewhere on your list of what's important. You are very neighborly with gophers."

"Gophers don't think of me as a service provider. Besides, the idea of doing service makes me squirm. I want to be helpful, but I don't want to "do service." It's a doing and being distinction. Get it?"

"I guess it's a command performance that you resist. Nevertheless, you may someday find yourself in need of neighborly neighbors."

"I'm in the here and now."

"Well, it's too late," Elder Plant announced.

"For what?"

"Relations that should have been cordial got chummy, and it's your fault for not doing boundary work. Say no, mean it, and then you don't have to be put out or perturbed about doing things you didn't want to do in the first place.

"Besides, Prissy, you are an outsider. Folks like you prefer the perimeter of social engagement. For goodness sake, acknowledge your preferences and relax."

"Relax …?" Prissy looked incredulous.

"Not everyone is meant to be in the thick of things. Be yourself."

"I thought you were going to tell me to suck it up and deal."

"I am."

"Yeah, but, my predicament isn't so cut and dried. My neighbors have human needs that tug at my heart-strings."

"My dear girl, get on with your life. The world will get on without you."

"But …"

"Prissy, you're getting on my nerves. You want to be happy, don't you?"

"Oh, I do."

"Then try to win some happiness and pass it on to other folks."

"Hey, I can do that!" Prissy exclaimed.

"Well that's good, because frankly Prissy, you'll need a saving grace or two to offset your, ah, reluctance to social accommodation."

"Isn't happiness grace enough?

# Chapter Nineteen: Normalized

My name is Perry. My nut cracked a couple of years ago when I was eighteen. Longitudinal dehiscence is what pomologists call it. And dehisce I did when I went nut to cranium with loony Stan, my Bone Head pal. Stan got a concussion; my endocarp split. And after that, there were folks who were all too willing to think of us as broken.

Our disagreement began when I took a progressive position and Stan countered with an off-the-wall conspiracy theory. Stan got all emotional and wouldn't listen. But on this particular day, I sorta insisted on being heard, and when Stan wouldn't shut up, I head-butted him. I'm not proud to admit this because an endocarp is harder and better suited for brain holding than a cranium. So, what I am saying is that, I knew that my nut could crack his cranium, and I did it anyway. I felt terrible. We went to the emergency room together and were admitted to the same hospital room.

Serves me right, I guess. I was assigned a couple of Bone Head physicians who didn't know diddley squat about what to do with a cracked endocarp. I guess it never occurred to them that nuts are made to crack—or that there's no cause for alarm unless my nut was bruised or busted, which it wasn't. Anyway, I let the doctors ponder my predicament, so that I could stick close to my pal.

My doctors gave me a complete neurological workup. I did not pass with flying colors. Diagnosis: Tourette syndrome. On top of that, Bone Heads in white jackets convinced my folks that my impulsive, compulsive, obsessive, and hyperactive self needed some ironing out. I would rather have sorted out my disorders with a P Head Elder, but mom and dad insisted that I go see a Bone Head specialist.

While Stan was hospitalized, his parents decided that his personality was an issue as well. When he was discharged, they hauled him off to a therapist who gave him medications that turned him into a loony zombie. It was sickening to watch. Mind you, before he was treated, Stan was no worse and no better than he'd ever been. And I know this because we grew up together. Stan was always a weird Harry, preoccupied with his appearance and given to emotional outbursts, but within his family and in our community, Stan's troublesome self was a non-issue.

Weeks later, when Stan and I finally reconnected, we compared notes. Stan announced, "I have a histrionic personality disorder."

"Really? I have Tourette's and other associated traits."

Silence.

"I am broken," Stan said.

"Nah, you just are what you are."

Silence.

"I lost my crazy confidence," Stan said.

"I admired your crazy confidence."

"Yeahhh," Stan said. "I thought I was okay."

That day Stan and I officially rejected the rubrics that others applied to our lives and the notion that being broken is a defining piece of your story. We agreed to be okay in our own way. With that, Stan flushed his meds down the toilet and I fired my psychiatrist. Who fires their therapist? Well, I did. I told her that she was too fixated on what was wrong with me. But, our determination not to be broken would be tested.

A month later, Stan got into a kerfuffle with some guy in front of Sweetie Pie's Bakery. The police came, cuffed him, and took him over to the Psychiatric Health Facility. Stan got a court-assigned social worker and was put back on meds. Not everybody appreciated Stan's worldview.

The next time I saw my friend, he looked a wreck. I jumped him and put him in a headlock. "Hey brother, you're not broken are you?"

Stan laughed from somewhere deep inside a drugged-out inertness. But honestly I couldn't tell if he was a mental case or if he was just an overmedicated zombie. I was so undone by his predicament that I went looking for a P Head Elder. Placerville has a few hundred P Heads and I found Dr. Perdue Psyches, a psychiatrist, who had a tiny office in an alley right off Placerville's historic Main Street.

"Is Psyches your real name? How weird is that?" I asked.

"Yeah, strange isn't it? Then again, I once knew a proctologist named Nesselrod. What's on your mind?"

I told Psyches all about Stan and asked him what he could do for him. Psyches said, "Oh, nothing special. We'll just try to cultivate positive emotions, engagement, and meaning. We'll talk."

"Psychotherapy?"

"No, just talk. Come see me, anytime after four o'clock."

A week later, Stan and I dropped in on Dr. Psyches. He asked us to join him outside on his deck where he served hot coffee and Peppermint Patties. The porch was crammed with really healthy looking plants and the late afternoon sun had everything all lit up.

Stan still looked like he was operating from behind a purple haze, but he was able to launch into his favorite subject: medieval armaments and torture devices. On and on he went and it got pretty interesting. Stan loved attention and Dr. Psyches was on the edge of his chair and looking right at him so as not to miss a word. When Psyches wanted to add something, he'd say, "Hold on Sonny, so I can talk now." And then Psyches would ask a question or make a point. Sometimes I piped up with, "Shut up Stan, so I can say something." Stan, who was programmed to deliver monologues, played along and so we had a pretty good conversation.

On the way out Psyches said, "You boys come see me again soon. I'm old and sometimes lonesome. All of my friends are old coots who piss and moan about their aches and pains. I am always up for talk about things I've never heard before. Thank you, Stan, for sharing your subject with me. And thank you, Perry, for your good company."

We'd been seeing Psyches every week for a month when Stan asked me, "Is Psyches psyching me out?"

"I don't think so."

"What's he doing?" Stan asked.

"Nothing."

"Hmmm. Maybe he doesn't think that I'm broken."

Stan's question got me to thinking, what was Psyches doing? I mean, he never asked any leading questions, never steered the conversation, and never lectured or offered advice. Nor did he ask for money. He was doin' nothing, just like he said he would.

Then I got to wondering, in our everyday lives do we really pay that much attention to what's wrong with folks? I looked at the folks in my life and realized that most of them were different in their own way and that I usually overlooked, enjoyed, or paid little or no attention to those differences. This morning for example, I had a delightful visit with Mrs. Po and her pug, while pretending not to notice her persistent eye blinking. It was, after all, the polite thing to do. My mechanic has a scar that rips right across his face and with that scary face he does spot-on impersonations. And then there's Stan whose histrionics keep me from getting too complacent.

Maybe, I thought, Psyches is a really polite P Head who makes his encounters with differences into an everyday occurrence. Maybe he is purposely normalizing his patient's peculiarities.

That sounded pretty civilized to me, but my thinking along these lines ran into a few snags. For example, there are clearly some differences that are too serious for folks to ignore. And, there are some differences that take some getting used to—like my nut head. But ultimately, I decided that normalizing differences was one of the nicest things that we can do for someone. And, I guess Stan and I had the right idea when we decided not to be broken by our peculiarities.

# Chapter Twenty:
# Miraculous Biology

Paden, a Pistachio Head, and Joey, a human Bone Head, are twelve-year-olds who have been best friends for the past two years. Between them brotherly love is much in evidence—until it's not.

It's not brotherly love when Joey turns on Paden: "You are a stooopid nut head. Your brain is nutmeat. And, what kind of a freak has nutmeat for a brain?"

Paden is offended by Joey's outbursts, but he never retaliates. He was brought up to believe that name-calling is never acceptable.

When Paden finally decided that he'd had enough of Joey's putdowns, he went to see Pierre the Pontificator. P Heads are encouraged to seek the counsel of Elders regarding interpersonal perturbations. Elders mostly listen, rarely offer suggestions, and often manage to influence a situation without looking like they did a thing.

Paden told Pierre the Pontificator his story from start to finish.

"Well, darn. I am very sorry to hear that. Hmmm … I know Joey. Why don't you invite him to our next *P Heads Under The P Tree Event*. But in the mean time, don't you do anything different because you are fine just as you are. Splendid in fact; you are a splendid boy."

"Oh, okay … thanks, Mr. Pontificator."

A week later, on a perfect summer day, a group of mostly P Heads gather under their community pistachio tree to picnic and talk about what's important. Conversation is lively throughout the afternoon, but as the sun begins to set, folks quiet down and get ready for story time. Today, the storyteller is old bird toes himself, the much revered, Pierre the Pontificator.

Pierre arrives and sits down in the story chair with his back to the setting sun. He spots Paden, his family, and Joey Jacobs sitting in the back. "Joey, will you please come forward to receive today's story?"

Surprised to be chosen, Joey scrambles over folks to reach Pierre.

"Joey, when Pistachio Heads ask a Bone Head to receive a story, it is an offering of friendship, a ritual that makes you our forever friend. Most of the folks in this audience have heard today's story, so they will listen in, and their presence is also an offering of friendship.

"Please put your chair across from mine and to the right. There, that's perfect. Now then, we'll wait for the crepuscular light to cast an amber glow over my shoulders and onto your faces. Ahhhh, here it is … bask in the glow of this golden moment. Pause. Now, son, tell us your full name."

"Joey Jay Jacobs."

"Joey Jacobs, I am Pierre the Pontificator. I am old, and my nut is packed with story stuff. Would you like to know about how Pistachio Heads came into Being?"

"Sure."

"Our story begins with pistachio trees because we were originally meant to be trees. Every year in the fall, healthy pistachio trees grow hundreds of nuts that want to be trees. As soon as those nuts are fully grown, the mother tree drops them like hot potatoes. But, it's not all nicey nicey when they hit the ground. The lucky nuts get planted and germinate. Others get eaten by birds, harvested by humans, or lie around for years like zombies. Many end up pushing daisies. But here's where our story gets interesting: a handful of nuts will lose touch with their biological imperatives in order to become the ones who are neither this nor that."

Joey looked bewildered. "Do you mean not a human ... not a nut?"

"Exactly. But, we don't mind being an indeterminate species, and I am about to pontificate on that very subject."

"In the beginning, we were heads without bodies. Yes, in fact, we rolled around without bodies for quite some time. And I can tell by the expression on your face that you've never heard of such a thing. But, thousands of years ago, people in Iran, Turkey, and Afghanistan harvested pistachios from wild trees. Their children loved to roll the nuts around in their pockets and in the palms of their hands. Some of the children saw pistachios as little heads, drew faces on the shells, and made them into imaginary playmates."

"They imagined them as human ... heads?" Joey asked.

"Yes, and the children loved their little nut heads. In fact, being loved by children made pistachio nutmeat quicken with human emotions. By way of wishful think-ing on the part of the children, and with an extraordi-nary bursting forth of cells, pistachio nuts popped into Being. Let me be clear, they literally re-imagined their nuts into brain-holders and imagined human/vegeta-ble brains to go inside."

Joey's eyes went wide. "Just by imagining?"

"Yes, it's amazing. But, I bet you are wondering how can two species, a plant and an animal, combine to become something else? And maybe, you are won-dering what good is a head without a body?"

"Yeah," Joey interrupted. "And, if they could imag-ine a head, why not imagine a body?"

"Well … there are plenty of things that we don't know about how P Heads evolved. But," Pierre contin-ued, "we became more than just heads. It happened when the children fashioned body parts out of pieces of linen and wood and attached them to their nuts. And P Heads said to their heads, "Ouuuu yeah!" It was a voilà moment because a body is such a useful thing to have on hand. And it took some doing, but P Heads finally manifested a child-sized head and a body with all the fixings: blood, guts, muscles, bones, and private parts. But … our hybrid ancestors never quite perfect-ed that union of opposites. I mean look at us. We are an odd combination."

"You look okay to me."

"Oh, thanks for saying that, Joey, but in the final analysis, we look a bit unbelievable. But, that's all right, because being *unbelievable* is a state akin to a miracle.

"Miraculous biology is what we call it. But, you may be wondering why P heads didn't go Bone Head all the way. The truth is that we are pleased as punch with our hybrid nature. Upstairs we are more nut than human and we make no bones about it. In fact, we consider being nutty a valuable perspective on life.

"But, that's enough story for now. And Joey, as our forever friend, you are always welcome to join us when we gather under the P tree to talk about what's important.

"I want to thank Joey Jay Jacobs, for receiving our story, and the audience for listening in. May your lives be rich in friendship."

Folks lit their lanterns, collected their belongings, and headed for home. Pierre the Pontificator, Paden, and Joey led the procession. When they reached the edge of town, Joey asked, "Mr. Pontificator, are P Head brains better than … Bone Head brains?"

"Oh my, no. A brain is a brain."

"But, Pistachio Heads have magic."

"Oh no, no. It's the Maker that makes our story look magical. It's the Maker who engineers patterns of genetic expression. Evidence of miraculous biology is everywhere in our universe."

"But," Joey insisted, "P Heads shape shifted … right?"

"Ahhhh … well … kind of. We think of it as a redeployment of genetic potential."

"Wow, that's a cool story, Mr. Pontificator."

Joey turned to Paden and said, with all earnestness, "All this time I thought your brain was nut meat."